# TIPPING POINT

## LANTERN BEACH MAYDAY, BOOK 3

### CHRISTY BARRITT

# COMPLETE BOOK LIST

**Squeaky Clean Mysteries:**

#1 Hazardous Duty

#2 Suspicious Minds

#2.5 It Came Upon a Midnight Crime (novella)

#3 Organized Grime

#4 Dirty Deeds

#5 The Scum of All Fears

#6 To Love, Honor and Perish

#7 Mucky Streak

#8 Foul Play

#9 Broom & Gloom

#10 Dust and Obey

#11 Thrill Squeaker

#11.5 Swept Away (novella)

#12 Cunning Attractions

#13 Cold Case: Clean Getaway

#14 Cold Case: Clean Sweep

#15 Cold Case: Clean Break

#16 Cleans to an End

While You Were Sweeping, A Riley Thomas Spinoff

## The Sierra Files:

#1 Pounced

#2 Hunted

#3 Pranced

#4 Rattled

## The Gabby St. Claire Diaries (a Tween Mystery series):

The Curtain Call Caper

The Disappearing Dog Dilemma

The Bungled Bike Burglaries

## The Worst Detective Ever

#1 Ready to Fumble

#2 Reign of Error

#3 Safety in Blunders

#4 Join the Flub

#5 Blooper Freak

#6 Flaw Abiding Citizen

#7 Gaffe Out Loud
#8 Joke and Dagger
#9 Wreck the Halls
#10 Glitch and Famous

**Raven Remington**
Relentless 1
Relentless 2 (coming soon)

**Holly Anna Paladin Mysteries:**
#1 Random Acts of Murder
#2 Random Acts of Deceit
#2.5 Random Acts of Scrooge
#3 Random Acts of Malice
#4 Random Acts of Greed
#5 Random Acts of Fraud
#6 Random Acts of Outrage
#7 Random Acts of Iniquity

**Lantern Beach Mysteries**
#1 Hidden Currents
#2 Flood Watch
#3 Storm Surge
#4 Dangerous Waters
#5 Perilous Riptide
#6 Deadly Undertow

**Lantern Beach Romantic Suspense**

Tides of Deception

Shadow of Intrigue

Storm of Doubt

Winds of Danger

Rains of Remorse

Torrents of Fear

**Lantern Beach P.D.**

On the Lookout

Attempt to Locate

First Degree Murder

Dead on Arrival

Plan of Action

**Lantern Beach Escape**

Afterglow (a novelette)

**Lantern Beach Blackout**

Dark Water

Safe Harbor

Ripple Effect

Rising Tide

**Lantern Beach Guardians**

Hide and Seek

Shock and Awe

Safe and Sound

**Lantern Beach Blackout: The New Recruits**

Rocco

Axel

Beckett

Gabe

**Lantern Beach Mayday**

Run Aground

Dead Reckoning

Tipping Point

**Crime á la Mode**

Deadman's Float

Milkshake Up

Bomb Pop Threat

Banana Split Personalities

**The Sidekick's Survival Guide**

The Art of Eavesdropping

The Perks of Meddling

The Exercise of Interfering

The Practice of Prying

The Skill of Snooping

The Craft of Being Covert

## Saltwater Cowboys
Saltwater Cowboy

Breakwater Protector

Cape Corral Keeper

Seagrass Secrets

Driftwood Danger

## Beach House Mysteries
The Cottage on Ghost Lane

## Carolina Moon Series
Home Before Dark

Gone By Dark

Wait Until Dark

Light the Dark

Taken By Dark

## Suburban Sleuth Mysteries:
Death of the Couch Potato's Wife

## Fog Lake Suspense:
Edge of Peril

Margin of Error

Brink of Danger

Line of Duty

**Cape Thomas Series:**
Dubiosity
Disillusioned
Distorted

**Standalone Romantic Mystery:**
The Good Girl

**Suspense:**
Imperfect
The Wrecking

**Sweet Christmas Novella:**
Home to Chestnut Grove

**Standalone Romantic-Suspense:**
Keeping Guard
The Last Target
Race Against Time
Ricochet
Key Witness
Lifeline
High-Stakes Holiday Reunion
Desperate Measures

Hidden Agenda

Mountain Hideaway

Dark Harbor

Shadow of Suspicion

The Baby Assignment

The Cradle Conspiracy

Trained to Defend

Mountain Survival

**Nonfiction:**

Characters in the Kitchen

Changed: True Stories of Finding God through Christian Music (out of print)

The Novel in Me: The Beginner's Guide to Writing and Publishing a Novel (out of print)

## CHAPTER ONE

KENZIE ANDERSON JERKED her eyes open, confusion muddling any coherent thought in her mind. Everything around her blurred. Felt unsteady. The pounding in her head made her want to disappear into unconsciousness again.

She blinked, trying to clear her thoughts as something internal urged her to not succumb to her body's desire to rest. But her vision remained blurred.

Moving her fingers, she felt something hard beneath her. Smooth. With subtle ridges.

Wood? Maybe.

Her body swayed back and forth as if she were a baby being rocked by her mama.

But her mom had been dead for far too long, and

Kenzie most definitely was no longer a baby. So why was she rocking?

With every new question that filled her mind, nausea churned in her stomach. Something was seriously wrong.

As a spray of water hit her cheeks, more facts clicked into place—facts she'd rather ignore. Denial seemed safer than facing the truth.

Kenzie braced her arms beneath her and pushed herself up. As soon as she lifted her head, her mind swirled and she paused.

Her mouth was dry, and her tongue felt swollen.

Had she been drugged? It was the only explanation she could think of as to why she would feel this way.

Her entire body rocked again, along with the wood beneath her. The motion added to the swirling in her head and the nausea.

Quickly, Kenzie leaned over and spewed the contents of her stomach.

She slunk back down and wiped her mouth with the back of her hand, feeling like she could throw up again at any minute.

Instead, she forced herself to blink. Her vision *had* to clear. Nothing would make sense until it did. She had to see things with her own eyes.

Several blinks later, the world around her came more into focus.

Kenzie sucked in a salty breath of air.

She was on a boat. A small one. Probably only eight or nine feet. A naked pole rose at the center of the vessel, absent of any sail.

Her gaze stretched beyond the wooden stern.

The blood left Kenzie's face as she realized she was surrounded by nothing but water and angry waves.

Nausea welled in her again, and she leaned over the edge of the boat to throw up a second time.

Panic raced through her as reality continued to sink in.

She was in a boat without a sail, set adrift in what appeared to be the middle of the ocean.

How had she gotten here? How long had she been here, for that matter?

As the questions pummeled her, another wave hit the side of the boat and jostled it back and forth with a vengeance. Kenzie gripped the sides so she wouldn't tumble from the vessel.

She had no idea how to fix this situation.

But if she didn't, she wouldn't survive.

JIMMY JAMES FINISHED GETTING DRESSED and readied himself to head to the Lantern Beach Marina. He had two days before the next charter started, and he was trying to help out his friend and harbormaster, Stevie-o Peters, in the meantime.

Jimmy James had worked as a dockhand for the past several years, but his dream of becoming a captain had been accelerated when the former captain of *Almost Paradise,* a luxury yacht, had been found dead.

However, the last thing he wanted to do was to leave Stevie-o in a bind. Even though a local teen named Danny was helping out in his absence, Jimmy James wanted to do whatever possible to ease their workload. Besides, he liked to stay busy.

Just as he grabbed his keys and stepped toward the front door, his cell phone rang. He glanced at the screen and saw Police Chief Cassidy Chambers was calling.

He shoved his eyebrows together, wondering why she'd call this early. The two of them had certainly had ample opportunities to interact over the past few weeks as some suspicious activities had taken place at the harbor. But he thought all those issues had been resolved.

He put the phone to his ear and continued

outside, locking his cottage behind him. "Good morning, Chief."

"Hey, Jimmy James. Sorry to call so early. But I have a question that couldn't wait."

His curiosity peaked. "Sure, Chief. What's going on?"

"I had to work a case late last night and into the morning hours, and Ty's been out of town. But when I got back to the cottage this morning, I noticed Kenzie wasn't here."

His back straightened as the midmorning sunlight flooded him. "She wasn't there?"

"She could have left early to go to the docks, but her car is still parked under the house, and she hasn't been answering her phone. She's not with you, is she?"

He paused by his beat-up Dodge Ram. "No, she's not."

"Did she say anything to you about any plans?"

"The two of us hung out last night and had dinner. But then I took her back to her car and watched her drive toward your place. That was the last I heard from her."

"Good to know," Chief Chambers said. "I'm going to continue asking around, just so I can have some peace of mind. But you were clearly the first person I needed to start with."

He climbed into his truck and slammed the door. "I'm heading to the harbor now, so I'll also ask around. You might want to check with the rest of the crew. They've been hanging out at the campground in between our charters."

"I'll do that," Chief Chambers said. "And if you hear anything in the meantime, let me know."

"Will do." Jimmy James tossed his phone onto the seat beside him, his gut churning.

This wasn't like Kenzie.

Jimmy James had offered to drive her home last night. But Kenzie had insisted she'd be fine. He'd thought their troubles were finally behind them.

What if he'd been mistaken?

Wasting no more time, he took off down the road. He hoped the bad feeling in his gut was wrong —but it rarely was.

## CHAPTER TWO

*NO, no, no, no . . .*

Panic continued to bubble up inside Kenzie as the direness of her situation sank in. She leaned over the side of the boat just in case she threw up again. Water sprayed her face. In the distance, she heard the rumble of thunder, saw cracks of lightning split the sky.

She was going to die out here, wasn't she?

She squeezed her eyes shut. "Don't let your thoughts go there. Stay calm. And think. There's always a solution."

That's what her father had always told her. Those words had been his favorite mantra—and, as a surgeon, her dad turned them into a true lifesaver on many occasions.

But as she glanced around at the watery expanse stretching as far as the eye could see, no solutions came to mind.

Even if Kenzie found something to use as a paddle, she had no idea which direction to head.

"No, that's not true." She sat up straighter as her muddled thoughts cleared. "Look at the sun. That's what sailors did back before current navigation systems existed."

The sun peeked out beyond the clouds to the right of her. That must be the east.

Right? It was rising, not setting? Certainly, she hadn't been out here that long.

The last thing Kenzie remembered was pulling up to the cottage where she was staying. She'd climbed out of her car and headed toward the front door.

But before she could reach it—

Cold, hard fear ripped through her.

That was right.

Someone had lunged from the shadows, shoving a cloth over her mouth.

Then everything went black.

Now she was here. Certainly, twenty-four hours hadn't passed.

It only made sense that she was watching the sun

rise. Since the sun rose in the east, that meant
Kenzie needed to head in the opposite direction.

She was nearly certain this was the Atlantic
Ocean. The waves were too big to be the Pamlico
Sound. Besides, she'd most likely see land some-
where if she were in the sound.

Even though she'd now figured the direction,
that information still didn't help her get back to
land. Using her hand as a paddle wouldn't get her
very far. She had nothing to use as a sail. The boat
clearly had no motor.

That wasn't to mention the fact that those clouds
in the distance were dark. And they seemed to be
heading this way.

As if to offer confirmation, thunder rolled.

Her head sank between her arms as she fought
despair.

With any luck, maybe someone had realized she
was missing. Jimmy James. If anyone, he would have
noticed.

But she had this morning off to relax before their
next charter, and he was supposed to work at the
marina for Stevie-o. There was a good chance he
wouldn't notice her absence until later.

Maybe Cassidy had realized she hadn't been at
the house last night. Kenzie had been staying with

the police chief. Certainly, Cassidy would ask around. Maybe boats were out there right now searching for her.

Kenzie surveyed the area for any signs of hope. But the ocean was vast. Even if people were looking for her, who knew how long it would be until she was found?

The late summer sun already felt sweltering. Her skin was warm and dry, and her lips had cracked.

Not only that, but these waves were so much larger than what Kenzie was used to experiencing. If a wave hit this boat the wrong way, the vessel would reach a tipping point and Kenzie could be tossed overboard.

She closed her eyes as she tried to gather her thoughts.

*Think, Kenzie. Think.*

She sank lower into the boat. As she did, something hard dug into her backside.

She reached into her pocket.

Her fingers closed around the object, and she pulled it in front of her.

Her heart stammered as she stared at her cell phone.

Whoever had done this to her had left her cell phone? What sense did that make?

She wouldn't complain. Instead, she hit the screen. The device didn't turn on.

Strange. She rarely ever turned it off.

Kenzie held down the side button until the screen flashed on. Then she checked the upper righthand corner of the device.

She had ten percent on her battery. One bar of service.

If this boat drifted out any farther, she might not have any service.

Wasting no time, she pulled up her contacts and dialed.

JIMMY JAMES PACED THE DOCKS, the wood sun-bleached and littered with fish guts and bird droppings. He looked for any signs of Kenzie.

There were none.

No one had seen her or heard from her since yesterday.

Kenzie's car was still at Chief Chambers' house, and she hadn't answered her phone when he tried earlier.

The chief had called a few minutes ago to let Jimmy James know she'd gone to the campground to talk to the rest of the charter crew. But no one knew anything.

The bad feeling in Jimmy James' gut grew stronger by the moment.

Just then, his phone rang in his pocket. He paused near *Almost Paradise*, the charter boat he captained, and quickly pulled his cell from his pocket.

His pulse quickened when Kenzie's name appeared on his screen.

He shoved the phone to his ear as his heart raced. "Kenzie? Is that you? Where are you? We've all been worried."

The phone crackled with a bad connection. "Boat . . . middle of . . . help."

He paced, hoping to find a better signal. "What? Can you repeat that?"

"I'm on a boat . . . ocean."

Her words still weren't making sense. Kenzie was on a boat in the ocean? Why would she be on a boat? Especially without telling him?

"Please . . . find me."

His blood went cold at her words.

She wasn't on a boat out in the ocean by her own choice. Something was wrong.

His mind raced as he tried to formulate a plan.

"Is there anything around you, Kenzie? Anything that will give us an idea where you are?"

"Just . . . water."

His heart pounded harder as he glanced at the horizon. Today's forecasted storm looked like it was coming in faster than anticipated. Thunder seemed to growl in the distance, warning of what was to come.

"Phone's . . . about to . . . die."

His breaths became shallower. The situation seemed more dire every moment. Especially when he looked at the sky and saw the dark clouds there.

"Stay with me," he said. "I'm going to get backup. You hang in, you hear me?"

"I . . . hear . . ."

He jogged toward the marina office.

He didn't want to get off the phone with Kenzie. But he also didn't want to waste her battery. The police may be able to use it to ping her location.

He rushed into the office and grabbed the phone from Stevie-o's desk. Keeping Kenzie on the line, he called Chief Chambers. She promised to notify the Coast Guard and said she was on her way to the marina.

"Kenzie?" Jimmy James leaned against the desk,

anxious to tell her the update, to reassure her he'd help.

But only silence answered.

His gut lurched.

No!

Had her phone died? Or was she out of range?

Jimmy James couldn't say for sure.

But he was certain about two things. Kenzie was in grave danger, and he had to help her.

# CHAPTER THREE

KENZIE STARED AT HER PHONE, fighting the panic inside her.

The call had been dropped. No bars were left at the top of her screen.

Did that mean no one could trace her location?

She didn't know how that worked.

But this phone had been her only hope. Finding her out here in the ocean would be like finding a needle in a haystack, as the saying went.

What was she going to do now?

She bit back a cry of despair.

A brisk wind swept over the boat. At least the clouds offered some reprieve from the blistering sun.

But her chances were better at surviving the sun than they were at surviving a storm.

As she stared at the sky overhead, a squall stirred in the distance. The wind became stronger by the second. The sky darker. The waves larger.

Kenzie gripped the sides of the boat and squeezed her eyes shut. *Dear Lord, please help me. Please.*

Her prayer was simple and desperate. There was nothing else she could do except to beg for God's mercy right now.

Why would someone do this to her? Sure, she'd found herself unwittingly in the middle of solving two crimes recently. But the bad guys were now behind bars, so it made no sense why someone would target her like this now.

She scanned the boat again, but nothing had been left inside. No emergency flares or first aid kit or tools. The vessel was bare bones.

Maybe she could climb from the boat, hold onto the back, and use her legs like a motor to propel the vessel forward. Whatever happened, she couldn't risk being separated from the boat. She would never survive if she did.

She sighed. At least her idea was a possibility of *something* she could do to be proactive. Still, the move would be risky. Maybe a last resort.

She scanned the horizon again, hoping to spot another boat.

But there were none. Nothing. Just water.

If Kenzie were closer to the shore, fishermen and shrimp trawlers or maybe even the occasional military vessel or cargo ship might go by.

But the fact she saw no one only confirmed her fears that she was out far. Too far.

Her hope dwindled at the thought.

What if no one found her? How long would Kenzie survive on her own? And exactly what would eventually kill her?

Starvation? The sun? Ocean life?

Kenzie rubbed her arms.

It was better if she didn't think about it.

But not thinking about it didn't seem like an option right now.

---

"WE'VE TRIED to ping Kenzie's cell phone, but it's difficult. There aren't exactly any cell towers in the middle of the ocean, but we were able to get a location on the last place she had a signal."

Chief Chambers pointed to a five-mile area on the nautical map in front of them. She'd taken over the marina office as she commandeered the situation. Her blonde hair was pulled back into a bun, and her uniform barely concealed her pregnant belly. Even though she was young, Jimmy James knew from experience that she was capable.

Jimmy James stepped toward the door, tired of waiting—especially since that storm was almost on them. "I'm going to take my boat out. I have a better chance finding her out there than I do by standing here in the office waiting."

Chief Chambers touched her growing belly as if some kind of maternal instinct had kicked in. "But you don't know where you're going."

He pointed to the map. "I know Kenzie is in that general area. That's where I'll head."

The chief continued to stare at him. Jimmy James' gaze remained unwavering as he tried to make it clear no one would be able to stop him.

"There's a storm coming, and your boat's not that big. Maybe you should leave search-and-rescue efforts to the professionals," she finally said. "The Coast Guard and marine police are already on their way."

"There's no way I can live with myself staying here while Kenzie's in danger."

She frowned. "I figured you would say that, but I

had an obligation to warn you. Going out there right now is dangerous."

"I know. I'm willing to take that risk."

"I'm sure Ty would say the same thing in this situation," Chief Chambers muttered. Ty was her husband and a former Navy SEAL. "Listen, one of the Blackout guys—Gabe—has been doing a lot of training lately, learning how to fly a commercial-grade drone. He's going to see if he can spot anything."

"Can he do that with the approaching storm?"

"As long as the wind doesn't get above twenty knots, he says he can. But it's risky. Let's hope it works."

Hope pulsed inside him. "If you see anything . . ."

"I'll let you know. In the meantime, be careful. You won't be any good to Kenzie if you're injured or dead."

Jimmy James' chest tightened at her words. He wanted to argue, but he couldn't. Chief Chambers spoke the truth. If something were to happen to him, that would only pull emergency resources away from Kenzie. That wasn't what he wanted.

Which was why he had to find Kenzie without getting killed in the process.

# CHAPTER FOUR

AS THE BOAT continued to rock, Kenzie felt more nausea rising in her. She'd never been seasick before, so it had to be the mix of the small boat, the large waves, and whatever drugs she'd been given.

When she'd rubbed her arm earlier, she felt a tender spot on her bicep. After examining the area more closely, she saw a small prick mark.

After the person had grabbed her and knocked her out with something—chloroform was her best guess—he must have injected her with another drug to keep her sedated long enough to get her out in the middle of the ocean.

She tried to picture the whole thing unfolding.

She imagined the man—she assumed it was a man—had put her in a larger boat. Brought her to the middle of nowhere. Then dumped her in this smaller boat and left her here to die. Why not just dump her in the water? Would her death have been too quick?

Either way, someone who'd do something like that was cruel and calculated.

But why would someone that premeditated make the mistake of leaving her with her cell phone? That's what didn't make sense.

Kenzie leaned over the side of the boat and emptied the contents of her stomach again. There wasn't much left. She and Jimmy James had gone to a seafood restaurant last night, and she'd eaten a crab cake sandwich and fries.

The two of them had a really good time together. They'd hit a rough patch in their relationship last week and were still taking things slow. But she really enjoyed being around him. In fact, as Kenzie had told him good night and driven back to the cottage where she'd been staying, she'd felt so much hope blossoming inside her.

Stepping out on her own had been hard. Making her own way had been difficult.

But seeing her dreams within reach made everything worth it.

She glanced at the horizon as lightning lit the sky.

Now all those dreams were on the line.

Just as the thought filled her head, a gigantic wave rose across the ocean.

Her lungs froze as she watched it rising, rising, rising.

At any minute the water would crest.

The powerful surge was heading right toward her.

Her insides seemed to quiver.

Wasting no more time, she plunged her hands in the water and paddled. She had to turn the boat so the wall of water didn't hit her sideways. The small sailboat would certainly tip if it did.

Desperately, she stroked the water. But the turbulence beneath the surface had a mind of its own.

Still, she frantically paddled, not knowing what else to do. The wave grew and crested in the distance like a monster rising from the sea. Any minute now, the beast would hit her.

And Kenzie's boat still remained sideways.

"Come on!" Her muscles burned as she desperately tried to turn the boat at a forty-five-degree angle to the wave.

Before she could, her boat tilted. Rose. Almost felt suspended as the water captured it.

Then the wave crashed.

She tumbled, a mix of water and wood churning around her. She hardly knew which way was up as everything swirled together.

Moisture filled her nose.

As the ocean consumed her, Kenzie whispered desperate prayers.

---

"I'LL GO WITH YOU," someone yelled across the harbor.

Jimmy James glanced back and saw Stevie-o jogging toward him from the marina office. The man's reddish-brown beard glinted in the sun, and his sunglasses obscured his gaze.

The harbormaster was one of the best watermen Jimmy James knew.

Jimmy James didn't slow his steps as he headed across the gravel parking lot. "Are you sure?"

"I'm sure. If you find her, you're going to need a hand. Especially with a storm coming in."

Jimmy James motioned for his friend to follow. He couldn't argue with Stevie-o's assessment. His chances were better if he had someone to help him. Stevie-o was crazy enough to go out in this weather with him.

A few minutes later, the two of them were on Jimmy James' Bayliner headed out from the inlet toward the ocean. He knew the general area where Kenzie might be, but he realized it was a long shot he'd find her. Still, he had to try.

His boat already bucked in the waves. This was going to be a rough ride.

But he didn't care. Not if it meant finding Kenzie.

"Do you have any idea what happened?" Stevie-o stood beside Jimmy James at the helm, raising his voice to be heard over the roar of the motor.

Jimmy James shook his head as he gripped the wheel. "At this point, I have no clue."

"Have you tried her cell phone anymore?"

"My guess is that it's dead. It didn't have much battery left when Kenzie contacted me. Chief Chambers is still trying to pinpoint Kenzie's exact location, but she hasn't been able to do that yet."

Stevie-o nodded at the sky. "This isn't looking good. There's a small craft advisory out."

Jimmy James' jaw tightened. He already knew that. But hearing his friend say it aloud caused his heart to thrum harder. "I know. I'd say I could take you back, but you and I both know we don't have much time if we're going to find her."

"I knew the risk when I told you I'd come with you. Keep going." Stevie-o motioned with his hand for them to continue forward.

Jimmy James charged deeper into the ocean, praying he'd find Kenzie quickly.

He found some comfort in knowing that the Coast Guard and marine police were also looking for her. With all of them, maybe she would be located. But he had no idea what kind of boat she was on. A large one? Something closer to a dinghy?

Because if Kenzie was on a dinghy, a vessel like that wouldn't last long out in this weather. The waves were huge, at least fifteen to twenty feet high in places.

The water was only going to get rougher from here.

Jimmy James thought about Kenzie's sweet face. About the warm conversations they'd had since they'd been getting to know each other.

Last night had really felt like a turning point. The two of them just clicked. There was no other way to describe the connection growing between them.

Against all the odds, they were falling for each other.

Against the odds of Jimmy James being the bad boy and Kenzie being the good girl. Against the odds of Jimmy James coming from a poor family while Kenzie came from an affluent one. Against the odds that Kenzie had been in med school and he'd barely finished high school.

But, somehow, they worked.

Though he'd mistakenly let his doubts get the best of him and called things off with Kenzie earlier, Jimmy James had been praying they'd move beyond his snafu. He prayed that he could prove himself to her.

"Are we getting closer?" Stevie-o yelled above the roar of the wind, waves, and engine.

Jimmy James glanced at the pin on his phone's map. "We're still at least a mile out from the area I want to look at."

"A mile?" His voice rose in pitch.

Jimmy James knew exactly what Stevie-o was getting at.

The odds weren't looking good.

# CHAPTER FIVE

AS KENZIE'S face breached the water, she sucked in a quick breath. Her lungs screamed for air.

Another wave swept over her and plunged her beneath the water's surface again. She held her breath, fighting panic as the currents tugged at her. It felt as if the water had clamped around her legs and pulled her under.

She propelled her way up.

Still gasping for air, she treaded water. Her gaze scanned around her.

Where was her boat? Her odds of surviving were much greater with a floatation device than if she was out in the ocean on her own.

She didn't see the small sailboat anywhere.

The turbulent waters seemed to grasp at her

ankles and try to tug her under again, like a watery boogeyman claiming its prey.

More panic bubbled inside her.

No! Kenzie couldn't let the ocean win. She wasn't going to give up. Not yet.

But she needed to find that boat.

Kenzie glanced behind her, and her heart hammered into her chest.

Another monster wave was coming. If it shoved her under, she may not surface again.

Her energy was fading.

*What would Jimmy James tell her to do?*

Suddenly, an idea hit her. She and Jimmy James had gone to the beach two days ago. As they'd been in the water, he'd taught her the best way to get past the shorebreak and to the sandbar beyond.

Maybe she could use those tips now.

She dove under the water and swam toward the wave. She'd go beneath it and miss part of the strong currents.

She hoped.

Her lungs screamed as she kicked her legs and fanned out her arms.

Just a little farther.

Her lungs continued to burn, desperately wanting air.

Finally, she surfaced and gasped in a quick breath. Then she glanced behind her.

She'd done it. She'd missed the wave and come out on the other side!

But her relief was short-lived.

More waves were coming. How many times could she repeat what she'd just done before her body couldn't do it any longer?

Images of everyone she cared about flashed through her mind.

Jimmy James . . . she'd kept him at arm's length until she knew for sure she could trust him, that he wouldn't try to make decisions about her future as if she had no insight or choice herself.

Her dad . . . things hadn't ended well between them after their last conversation. What if that was the last time they ever talked?

A cry lodged in her throat.

This wasn't supposed to happen. She was supposed to have more time . . .

*Don't give up. It's not over until it's over. You've still got fight left in you.*

Wiping the water from her eyes, she glanced around.

Was that . . . something in the distance?

Her boat! That was her boat!

It was probably fifty feet away. Could she reach it?

The thunder and lightning overhead seemed to warn her that more danger was coming.

Kenzie had to try, at least.

Before all her energy depleted, she swam across the water, fighting the current with each stroke. But with every inch she moved toward it, the boat seemed to drift at least another foot away.

*No, Lord! Please, help me!*

Kenzie gulped in another breath. She had to try harder. She had no other choice.

Diving beneath the surface, she swam as quickly and as forcefully as she could. She had to reach the boat.

Because, right now, that vessel was her only hope of survival.

---

"WE'RE GOING to have to turn back soon," Stevie-o shouted against the wind as they continued to head into the heart of the storm.

Jimmy James gripped the throttle, his gaze set straight ahead. "Not yet. We can make it farther."

"These waves are going to tip us."

Rain slapped Jimmy James' face almost as if nature tried to knock some sense into him. But it wasn't going to work. "I'm not turning back yet. I'm sorry. Maybe you shouldn't have come."

Stevie-o used his fingers to push the water from his face. "No, I want to help. I just think we should have waited until after the storm passed."

Jimmy James' determination continued to grow stronger, despite his friend's words. "By the time the storm passes it might be too late for Kenzie, especially depending on her circumstances. I can't risk that."

"I understand."

"Here, take the helm." Jimmy James nodded toward the wheel.

As Stevie-o moved into place, Jimmy James grabbed his binoculars and scanned the horizon. He just needed *something*, some sign of hope.

Instead, he saw angry waves cresting like an unrelenting army.

His cell phone buzzed. He saw it was Chief Chambers and quickly put the device to his ear.

"You have an update?" His heart pounded with anticipation.

"Gabe's bringing his drone back in. The wind is too strong."

"Did he see anything?"

"He thinks he may have spotted a small boat in the water. I'm going to send you the location. But Jimmy James, I strongly advise that you get back to shore. The storm looks like a doozy."

Determination hardened his muscles. "Send the coordinates to me. Just in case I'm closer than the Coast Guard or the marine police."

She let out a soft, hesitant sigh. "I'll do that now. Be careful."

Jimmy James waited until the coordinates came through. The location was only about a half a mile away. He could make it there if he pushed hard enough.

He prayed this move would lead him to Kenzie. That she was still alive. That she was okay.

And he prayed that whoever had done this to her was ready for a fight.

Because anyone who'd hurt Kenzie like this deserved to pay.

## CHAPTER SIX

AS KENZIE SWAM through the water, she hit something hard.

She surfaced and sucked in another breath.

It was her boat!

The water had calmed just enough for her to reach it.

The vessel had capsized, but she could still cling to it. Maybe she could rest a moment. Regain her strength.

Even though her muscles felt weak and shaky, she managed somehow to climb onto the hull of the boat. She clutched the slick surface, knowing with clarity that letting go could be a fatal mistake.

Once the storm passed, maybe Kenzie could

figure out a way to flip the boat over and climb inside. But for now, she was just happy to have something to keep her afloat.

She glanced around again, her face and hair soppy wet with saltwater. Rain had started, coming down in sheets only to ease up for a moment and then pour down again.

If rescue crews came out in this weather, would they even see her? Visibility was horrible. Everything was a watery blur.

Waves continued to violently crash into her. She clung to the boat, but the wood was slippery and the surface uneven. There was little to grab onto.

Kenzie pressed her eyes shut again.

*Please Lord, help me.*

At this point, nothing she could do by her own power would save her.

A cry of despair left her lips, only to be drowned by the howling wind.

---

"WE'RE ALMOST THERE." Jimmy James held the binoculars to his eyes again and scanned the water. But it was nearly impossible to see anything. They only had their navigation system to rely on.

"After we reach this location, I really think we should head back." Stevie-o wiped moisture from his face and droplets from his beard. "I'm telling you that as a friend. We're not going to be able to search for Kenzie if we're dead."

Jimmy James wanted to argue with the assessment, but he knew he couldn't. His friend was right. These conditions weren't safe, especially for a small boat like his.

"There's one more area over there I want to check. Then we can head back. We'll let the bigger boats do their jobs."

Jimmy James thought he saw something white in the water, but he couldn't be certain. The conditions —the rain, the dark sky, the rough seas—could hardly be worse.

Stevie-o headed in the direction he pointed. As he did, Jimmy James kept the binoculars to his eyes and searched for any sign of life.

The closer they got, the more certain Jimmy James felt that he'd seen something drifting in the water.

Was that . . . a small boat?

That had capsized?

His heart hammered harder against his chest. If Kenzie had been on that boat, then she clearly wasn't on it anymore.

And if that was the case . . .

He wiped the water from his eyes and sucked in a deep breath.

No, Jimmy James couldn't allow his thoughts to go there. He didn't want to think about those possibilities.

But the facts in front of him were hard to ignore.

"That's definitely a boat," Stevie-o shouted over the wind. "It doesn't look good."

Jimmy James' jaw tightened. "Let's get closer and make sure."

As they zoomed toward the overturned vessel, he scanned the water, looking for anyone who may have been aboard and fallen out.

But he knew the chances of someone surviving in these conditions were slim to none.

Kenzie had just come into his life. Jimmy James still needed to prove himself to be someone she could trust, someone who wouldn't let her down. What if it was too late?

*No, don't think like that. Don't lose hope. It's all you've got right now.*

His breath caught as they neared the upside-down boat thrashing in the waves.

Jimmy James wiped the water from his eyes again as he strained for a better look.

It appeared someone was on top of the boat clinging for her life.

Kenzie.

# CHAPTER SEVEN

KENZIE COULDN'T HOLD on much longer. Her grip was fading. Her fingers hurt. She could hardly breathe. Every time she tried to suck in a breath, another wave knocked the wind out of her.

She never imagined the ocean being her grave. But she supposed there were worse places to die.

Her uncle had always said she had saltwater in her veins. Maybe that had been some type of premonition . . . except she didn't believe in premonitions.

"Kenzie?"

She tried to pull her eyes open. Certainly, she was hearing things. Perhaps right before death people became delirious. Or maybe the drug she'd been injected with had caused a hallucination.

She almost thought she heard Jimmy James.

But there was no way he could have found her in these conditions.

"Kenzie!"

She forced her eyes open as the voice became clearer. Maybe she wasn't imagining things.

She wiped her eyes and blinked, searching for the person whose voice she'd heard.

Her breath caught. Was she seeing things?

"Jimmy James?" she called.

"It's me." As his boat pulled alongside the overturned vessel she clung to, he tossed her a lifejacket. "Can you put this on?"

Jimmy James . . . he'd found her! She'd have to celebrate later.

Right now, Kenzie had to concentrate on survival.

She grabbed the jacket with one hand and carefully pulled it over each arm. After a few fumbling attempts, she managed to snap a buckle on the front with one hand while maintaining her hold on the boat with the other.

"Now give me your hand!" Jimmy James shouted.

She reached toward Jimmy James' outstretched hand, but it was no use. Her muscles felt like they'd turned to gelatin. If she let go of the boat, she'd slip back into the ocean.

"I . . . can't."

"Yes, you can. Just give me your hand, and I'll do the rest." He bobbed up and down with the boat and the ocean waves. Thunder crashed again.

Was that Stevie-o at the helm? Had he come with Jimmy James to help rescue her?

"You can do it," Jimmy James said again.

But could she?

Kenzie pulled herself up but slipped again. She gasped as she lost her grip and began slipping toward the water.

But her fingers caught the underside of the boat, and she jerked to a halt.

She looked up at Jimmy James and saw worry stretching his gaze.

The next instant, he straddled the side of his boat. Leaned out. Looked dangerously close to falling into the water himself.

He gripped a rope and tossed it to her. "Grab this."

But the thought of letting go of this boat terrified her. Even if she knew that grabbing the rope was the best choice.

"You can do it!" he told her again.

Kenzie drew in a breath. Then, using her last

ounce of strength, she released one lifeline and grabbed another one.

She grasped the rope with both hands, willing herself not to let go.

The next instant, Jimmy James swooped down and lifted her onto his boat. Quickly, he set her on the floor before cradling her in his arms.

"We've got to get out of here." He motioned to Stevie-o. "But you have no idea how glad I am to see you."

Just as he said the words, the boat rocked as a wave rammed into the side. More lightning flashed, and rain flooded the air with so much force that visibility was nearly zero.

Kenzie knew they weren't out of trouble yet . . . she prayed this rescue operation didn't get Jimmy James and the rest of them killed.

———

"LET'S get back to shore. Now!" Jimmy James continued to hold Kenzie. With one hand, he grabbed a blanket from a compartment and wrapped it around her, knowing it wouldn't stay dry for long. But at least it might help her for now.

He couldn't deny that the storm was getting

worse. They couldn't have come this far only for things to get messed up now. They had to get back to dry land.

Just as the thought went through his head, a wave crashed into them and water flooded the boat.

"It's not looking good!" Stevie-o's muscles bristled as he stood at the helm.

"If anybody can get us home, it's you," Jimmy James told him.

He held Kenzie tighter and kissed the top of her head. She had curled into a ball and nestled beside him on the floor. They were still getting wet, but it was safer here than on the bench seat at the back of the boat. The way this boat was flopping around, it would be entirely too easy for them to topple off.

"Jimmy James . . ." Apprehension strained Stevie-o's voice.

In all his years of working with Stevie-o, Jimmy James wasn't sure he'd ever heard his friend sound so worried. He knew it had to be bad.

"We're taking on too much water," Stevie-o said.

Jimmy James could attest to the fact that at least four inches of water had accumulated on the bottom of his boat. The bilge pump should handle it . . . but would it drain in time? More water was sloshing inside by the moment.

"Jimmy James . . ." Kenzie muttered.

"It's okay. We're going to get you out of this."

The rain broke for a moment, and he glanced around. The waves were like walls around them—enormous, crashing walls.

For the first time, he wondered if they'd be able to escape this storm intact.

"You'll never believe this . . ." Stevie-o muttered.

At the ominous sound of his friend's voice, Jimmy James braced himself for the worst.

## CHAPTER EIGHT

KENZIE FELT JIMMY JAMES' muscles tighten and knew something was wrong.

She clung to him, afraid if she let go that she might slip back into the tumultuous water. As the thought rushed her mind, a wave crashed over the side of the boat, dousing them in saltwater.

"What's going on?" Kenzie stared at Stevie-o, trying to read his expression.

Stevie-o's words had scared her more than she wanted to admit. Her only regret was that Jimmy James had risked his life to save her. What were they going to do now?

"It's the Coast Guard." Stevie-o lowered his binoculars and nodded toward something in the distance.

As he did, the wind swept over them, spraying them with more water.

Kenzie's heart lifted. Had she heard him correctly?

She raised her head enough to see.

Sure enough, a Coast Guard vessel headed toward them. The cutter was large enough to withstand this kind of weather, a much safer bet than Jimmy James' Bayliner.

A cry of gratitude escaped from her lips. *Thank You, Jesus!*

A few minutes later, the cutter pulled up beside them and a coastguardsman issued instructions. Jimmy James carefully helped transfer Kenzie to the larger boat as huge waves swelled beneath them.

While Jimmy James and Stevie-o helped secure the Bayliner so it could be pulled behind the cutter, she was ushered into the cabin. Someone placed a dry blanket around her shoulders and checked her vitals. Reassured she was in stable condition, they handed her a bottle of water.

Finally, Jimmy James joined her and she felt safe again.

Thanks to Jimmy James, she hadn't died out there. But Kenzie was well aware of how close she'd come.

For now, she rested her head on Jimmy James' thick shoulder and waited to get back to dry land.

———

JIMMY JAMES never wanted to let go of Kenzie. Especially after what they experienced today.

He kept his arm around her as a coastguardsman questioned her about her ordeal. She hardly sounded like herself as she recounted each detail.

The more he learned about what happened, the more his anger grew.

How could someone do this to her? And why?

As the boat continued to rock, Jimmy James pulled his arm tighter around her shoulders. The two of them hadn't had a chance to talk since being rescued. Kenzie was being questioned and too many people milled around. But he was anxious to have a heart-to-heart with her, to find out how she was really doing right now.

His jaw tightened as he remembered how much differently things could have turned out today. He should have offered to drive Kenzie back to Ty and Cassidy's place last night. But he hadn't wanted to be pushy.

He hadn't wanted to make one mistake, which in

turn had led him to make a different mistake. He frowned. He needed to ensure that didn't happen again.

Just as they reached the Lantern Beach harbor, the storm began to clear. The water calmed, some of its anger dissipating. The rain dried up. The thunder became softer, more distant.

"You ready to get back on dry land?" he murmured to Kenzie as the crew docked the boat.

Her gaze fluttered to his, and she nodded. "Ready to be safe? Absolutely yes."

The next hour was a flurry of activity and official reports. The marina office remained command central, and the cup of coffee she'd been given seemed to comfort her.

Finally, Chief Chambers turned to Kenzie. "I want to get you to the clinic to be checked out."

Kenzie shivered, still looking scary pale. "That won't be necessary."

"We need to find out what they injected you with." Chief Chambers cut to the chase.

Kenzie's expression stilled as she seemed to realize the truth. "Of course."

Chief Chambers glanced at Jimmy James, and her voice softened with compassion as she asked, "Can you drive her there? I'll meet you."

Jimmy James nodded, almost a little too quickly. "Of course. Whatever you need to find who did this to her."

He led Kenzie to his truck and made sure she was safely inside before climbing in himself. He cranked the engine but, before putting the truck in Drive, he turned to her.

One look, and Kenzie crumpled into his arms. He held her close, wishing he could take away all her shock over her ordeal.

But he couldn't. He could only help hold her up and support her right now.

He ran his hand over her back, trying to soothe her. "I'm so sorry this happened to you, Kenzie."

"Thank you for coming to find me. I knew if anyone could do it, it was you." She sniffed as if holding back her emotions.

Kenzie's words brought him a strange comfort. Despite everything that happened between them, maybe she really did think the two of them had a chance. Jimmy James wanted her to know without a doubt that he'd always be there for her.

He continued to hold her until she pulled away and stared out the window, a forlorn look in her eyes.

Then he set off for the clinic.

# CHAPTER NINE

WHILE DOC CLEMSON treated Kenzie at the Lantern Beach Medical Clinic, Kenzie sent Jimmy James to pick up something for her to eat. She'd been allowed to use a shower at the clinic and Cassidy had found some clothes in her car that fit Kenzie.

With that done, Kenzie realized just how famished she was. Vending machine goodies weren't going to cut it.

Chief Chambers joined them in the exam room. As Kenzie remained on the exam table, she ran through the story again. But everything felt surreal, like she'd just woken up from a nightmare.

Her sunburn proved the ordeal had really happened, as did her chapped lips and tender arm.

Kenzie had been certain she was going to die out there. Bile churned in her gut at the thought, but she pushed those memories aside for now.

She couldn't let herself fully think about what had happened or she might break down. She had to hold herself together until she was alone.

Cassidy stood in front of her, notepad in hand and her face pinched with concern. As she addressed Kenzie, Doc Clemson typed some notes into his computer, giving them a moment.

"Kenzie, do you have any idea who did this?" Cassidy started.

Kenzie shook her head as she rubbed the goosebumps on her arms. She reminded herself to hold her emotions at bay. But her quivering voice was like a lid on the teapot rattling as water boiled inside.

"I have no idea," she finally said. "Really, I thought I'd put all this . . . this danger behind me."

"We all did."

"I was clearly targeted. Somebody wanted me to die." Kenzie's throat burned as she said the words. But her breath caught when she realized her statement wasn't necessarily true.

"What is it?" Cassidy leaned toward her, one hand going to her pregnant belly.

Kenzie pressed her lips together in thought,

contemplating what she had to say next. "There's one thing that doesn't make any sense to me. Whoever put me in that boat left me with my phone, almost like he wanted to give me a fighting chance to survive."

Cassidy narrowed her eyes. "When Jimmy James told me you'd called, I thought that was curious also. Was there anything else on your phone that maybe he wanted you to find?"

Kenzie hadn't even thought of that. "I didn't have much battery, and I didn't want to waste what I did have. I'm not sure if anything was on it."

"Where is your phone?"

"Amazingly enough, it stayed in my back pocket throughout everything. It's over there with my wet clothes. Even though it has a waterproof case, I'm not sure what kind of shape it's in. It's definitely dead right now. So I don't know if you'll find anything on it."

Cassidy strode across the room, took a plastic evidence bag from her pocket, and slipped the phone inside. "I'll take it back to the office to see if we can get it working. We need to check if there's anything on it, just to be certain."

"Whatever you need."

Cassidy paused and let out a breath as she

turned to Kenzie. "If you remember anything else . . . let me know, okay?"

Kenzie nodded. "I will. How long will it take to get the blood test back?"

"We should know something by tomorrow." Doc Clemson turned from his computer, tugging at the stethoscope around his neck as he addressed her question. "In the meantime, drink lots of water. Rest. Put a little aloe on your sunburn. But you should be okay."

Relief flooded her. "Thank you. I'm definitely grateful to be alive."

A knock sounded at the door, and Kenzie looked up to see Jimmy James there with a paper bag of food from Kenzie's favorite restaurant—The Crazy Chefette. The scent of melted cheese and toasted bread filled the room.

Her breath caught. She was so glad to see him. So glad to have him in her life.

But she had some big decisions to make in the near future.

———

JIMMY JAMES FELT a rush of nerves wash through him as he pulled to a stop in front of his cottage an hour later. Kenzie had stayed at the clinic long enough to quickly eat and fill out some paperwork. Then she'd been released.

As he glanced at Kenzie and noticed her staring at his house, Jimmy James wondered what she was thinking.

Even though they'd been hanging out, Jimmy James hadn't wanted to bring Kenzie here. He knew she wasn't the shallow type, but he still couldn't help but think she might judge him based on his humble accommodation.

The house was small and relatively unimpressive. But he kept it neat. The outside was nothing fancy. Then again, in this beach community, most people didn't have manicured lawns or flowerbeds.

Jimmy James had been so proud the day he'd saved up enough money to buy this place. A place of his own. He'd worked hard to get to this point.

"So, this is where you live?" Kenzie finally said, turning to glance at him.

"It's home sweet home."

"It looks really cozy."

As another ripple of nerves danced down his spine, he chided himself. He needed to stop being so ridiculous. He could captain a boat and lead a crew, but something about Kenzie Anderson seeing his house made him feel anxious.

Maybe it was because her opinion of him was important and no one else's mattered as much.

He cleared his throat. "Let's get you inside."

"You don't have to do this, you know." Kenzie cast him a knowing look.

"I don't have to, but I *want* to. Someone has to keep an eye on you." Jimmy James really didn't trust anyone else to do the job.

She nibbled on her bottom lip as she studied his face. "I just hate for you to feel obligated."

"Obligated? I don't feel obligated. Honored." He placed a hand on his heart.

Kenzie stared at him another moment as if trying to measure his words before finally offering a weak smile. "Okay then. Let's get inside."

Jimmy James hopped from the truck and ran around to meet her. He kept a hand on her elbow as he led her inside.

Standing by the front door, he held his breath as he waited for her reaction.

Kenzie glanced around, soaking everything in, before she finally nodded. "This place has potential."

"Potential?"

She took another step, her gaze still sweeping the space. "I mean, it's not really my style. But it has good bones. With the right paint, decorations, and furniture . . . it could be a real winner."

He wasn't sure why he felt so relieved to hear that. But he did. He wanted their lives to fit together. Now. In the future. Forever.

He swallowed hard. He'd never admitted that before. But he knew it was true.

A future without Kenzie didn't seem nearly as bright or happy.

"Why don't you have a seat and put your feet up? Do you need something else to eat?" As the questions rushed from him, Jimmy James wished he could stop them. But his lips seemed to have taken on a mind of their own.

Kenzie let out a laugh. "I'm fine."

Maybe Jimmy James was going a little overboard. But how could he not after what happened? He'd almost lost her today. Nothing about that was okay.

Their gazes caught. The next instant, she was in his arms, her head buried in his chest.

He heard a soft cry escape from her lips. Felt her shake. Knew she was crying.

He ran a hand across her back, his heart aching with compassion. He would do anything to take away this trauma. To have been the one out there today instead of her.

"It's okay," he murmured. "You're safe now."

"I thought I was going to die out there, Jimmy James."

Emotions clogged his throat, and he held her tighter. "I know. I'm sorry."

As she swayed in front of him, he scooped her into his arms and carried her to the couch. He set her there before lowering himself beside her, his gaze never leaving hers.

He sensed she'd been holding everything inside, not wanting to break down in front of everyone. But he was honored that she trusted him enough to grieve in his presence.

Even as they sat on the couch, she still clung to him. He gave her all the time she needed to process, to think, to either pull herself together or fall apart —whichever she needed.

After a moment, she drew away slightly, using the back of her hand to wipe away her tears. "While I was out there, I felt like I had this moment of clarity, this moment where I could see everything I needed to change—if I didn't die."

"Okay . . ."

Her watery gaze softened as it locked with his. "You were a part of that."

"Was I?" His breath caught. "What would you change with me?"

"I'd do this." She reached up and pressed her lips against his.

The tension left his shoulders as her soft hands brushed his neck. He pulled her closer as their kiss deepened. More than anything, he wanted to show her how much she meant to him.

As the passion between them seemed to explode, everything else disappeared.

If Jimmy James had his way, he'd never let her go.

# CHAPTER TEN

KENZIE'S HEART FELT FULL. Really full—despite everything that had happened.

She and Jimmy James had made dinner together. He'd taught her how to properly cook clams and crab legs. They'd eaten, talked, laughed, kissed some more.

Then they'd settled on the couch to unwind. Jimmy James had pulled her feet into his lap as they watched the movie *Overboard* on TV. The evening had been the perfect distraction for her earlier trauma.

"Kenzie . . ." Jimmy James' voice sounded hoarse as he turned toward her halfway through the movie.

She looked up at him, knowing by the tone of his

voice that whatever he was about to say was important. "Yes?"

He pushed a hair from her eyes. "Have you ever thought about going back to Delaware?"

Her muscles tensed, and she pulled back, not liking where she anticipated this conversation would go. "We're not going to have this discussion again, are we?"

"I'm just worried about you." His warm, concerned eyes locked on hers. "Somebody seems to be targeting you for no good reason. I can't help but think you'd be safer if you were back home."

She crossed her arms over her chest. "Safer? Maybe. But happier? No. I don't want to go back there."

"I'm afraid that as long as you stay here—"

"I have nowhere else to go."

He grabbed her hand. "You're a smart girl. I'm sure you could figure out something."

"If I didn't know better, I'd think you were trying to get rid of me."

His face softened. "The last thing I want is to get rid of you. I want to keep you around here forever."

His eyes widened as if he didn't mean to spill that truth.

But his words brought a surge of warmth through Kenzie's heart.

Jimmy James really was taking their talk seriously, wasn't he? A relationship with Kenzie wasn't a game or a fling. He honestly cared about her.

"I know you're worried about me," she started. "I'm worried too. But I'm not going to let the person behind this win. Besides, there's no guarantee that this guy won't follow me wherever I go. Until we know who's behind these acts and what his intentions are, it's really hard to make any kind of choice."

Just as she said the words, Jimmy James' phone rang and he glanced at the screen. "It's Chief Chambers."

He put the phone on speaker as he answered.

"Hey, Jimmy James," Cassidy said. "Is Kenzie with you?"

"She is. I have her here on speaker, but I can let you talk to her privately if that's what you guys want."

"Whatever you have to say, Jimmy James can hear it also," Kenzie said.

"I have good news and bad news. The good news is that we were able to get your phone working."

"That is good news." Kenzie certainly couldn't afford a new one right now.

"And the bad news?" Jimmy James asked.

"The bad news is that when we searched the notes section on your phone, we found a message that was written last night at 11:32 p.m."

The notes app was something Kenzie often used to jot down little reminders to herself. But 11:30 last night would have been during the time she had been abducted.

Her breath caught at the realization.

"What did it say?" Kenzie rushed.

"Just two words. Go home."

---

AS THE EVENING WOUND DOWN, Jimmy James reluctantly took Kenzie back to Cassidy and Ty's cottage. Thankfully, Cassidy and Ty were two of the most capable people Jimmy James knew. Still, he wished that somehow it wouldn't be inappropriate for her to stay at his cottage.

Kenzie lingered at the doorway, the sound of the waves crashing on the other side of the dunes filling the air. After her ordeal today, he wondered if the noise brought her comfort or fear.

"What's the plan for tomorrow?" Kenzie looked up at him, some of the color returning to her cheeks as the yellow glow of the porch light illuminated her face.

"Tomorrow?" Jimmy James stared at her, unsure what she was talking about.

"For *Almost Paradise*. Aren't we supposed to leave in two days?"

He shook his head, trying to find the right words to say in order not to sound bossy or like he was trying to control her life. "If you want to sit this one out, I'm sure we can—"

Fire lit in her gaze. "I'm not sitting this charter out. This is my job. Everyone is counting on me. And I want to do this."

Jimmy James nodded, knowing it would do no good to argue. In fact, that's what he'd expected Kenzie to say. He'd just hoped he could keep her away from danger somehow. However, there were no guarantees Delaware would be safe either.

"If that's what you want." He used a finger to tenderly push a hair from her eyes. "It's your choice."

"It is what I want." She paused as she stared up at him. "Do you want to come in? It looks like Cassidy and Ty are home."

He shook his head. "I would. But I have something I need to do."

Kenzie raised her eyebrows but didn't ask any questions.

"I just need to go back down to the harbor for a while," he finally said.

"I understand." She reached up and planted a kiss on his cheek. "Thank you again for everything that you did."

He caught her before she stepped back then leaned in for another quick but intoxicating kiss. "Call me if you need me."

"I will."

He waited until she was safely inside before he walked back to his truck and headed to the docks.

He had more questions he desperately needed answers to. There was no time like the present to see what he could dig up.

# CHAPTER ELEVEN

CASSIDY AND TY were waiting for Kenzie when she stepped into the cottage. After a few minutes of chitchat, they insisted she sit on the couch to relax.

Ty brought her some hot chocolate and freshly baked chocolate chip cookies as Kujo, their golden retriever, jumped beside her. The canine leaned closer as if he sensed Kenzie needed comforting—and maybe she did.

As Kenzie nibbled on her cookies, she couldn't help but reflect on how Ty and Cassidy were so nice and seemed so happy. Their relationship was exactly what Kenzie wanted one day for herself. If she ever married, she wanted a partner who respected her. Who let her have freedom to be herself while encouraging her to be her best.

Finding someone like that would be a rare gift. But Kenzie had wondered on more than one occasion if Jimmy James could be that person. He was protective, attentive, patient.

But still, it was too early to know.

"Oh, by the way, here's your phone. I have to admit, I'm surprised it still works." Cassidy stood, grabbed something from her leather bag, and handed it to Kenzie. "We checked it for prints and ran diagnostics on it. The only thing that we found was that message in your notes."

Kenzie took the phone before pulling the blanket back around her on the couch. "I still can't believe this guy left the phone with me. It seems like there were other ways he could have sent me that message—not that I'm complaining. The fact he left my phone helped me to be found."

"It is strange." As Cassidy sat down beside Ty, his arm stretched behind her.

"You said you haven't noticed anyone following you?" Ty asked. "You haven't had any strangers talk to you or anything else out of the blue happen?"

Kenzie shook her head. "No, there's been nothing."

Cassidy frowned and stared off in the distance a moment as if thinking. "We're going to keep looking into this until we know what happened. I'm just sorry for all you had to go through."

"Me too. But I'm glad I had a happy ending."

Ty leaned forward, the former Navy SEAL looking almost fatherly. "But you still need to remain on guard until we know exactly what is going on."

Kenzie didn't think she'd be able to forget that, even if she wanted to.

Part of her *did* want to quit before this next charter. But then she'd just be sitting around thinking about what happened. It was better, instead, if she stayed busy.

Besides, on the charter, Jimmy James would be there.

And she never felt as safe as she did when he was around.

"NO, I haven't seen anything suspicious." Leroy Leblon, one of the commercial fishermen who often utilized the marina, told Jimmy James as he stood on the docks washing down his boat after an evening fishing trip. "I'm sorry, man. I've mostly been focused on putting food on the table."

Jimmy James couldn't fault the man for that.

He nodded his thanks before continuing down the docks. Darkness hung in the air, and the harbor was mostly quiet except for a few boaters who were just getting back.

The more people Jimmy James could speak with, the better.

If someone had left Kenzie out in the ocean, this person would have launched their boat from somewhere close. This harbor made the most sense since it was the only one on the island. Taking Kenzie to a different location would have been too risky and taken too much time.

However, some people did keep their boats docked on the water by their homes, and there were two other smaller boat launches where somebody could have taken her.

Either way, Jimmy James was determined to get to the bottom of things and figure out who had done this to Kenzie.

He paused on the dock in front of *Almost Paradise*. Captaining a boat of this size had been quite the experience and, in many ways, had cemented in his mind that this was what he wanted to do.

Jimmy James had set up a plan for his future, one that included getting his own boat and doing charters bigger than the smaller fishing excursions he currently did in between his work as a dockworker. He wanted a better life for himself. A bigger nest egg so he didn't have to work from sunup to sundown until the day he died.

Plus, when he thought about Kenzie, she made him want to do better—be better—for his future as well. One day, he'd like to get married and be able to provide for a family. When he did that, it would be nice to have a schedule that allowed him to spend time with the people he cared about. Where he didn't have to work so much just to pay his bills.

Slowly, he was inching toward his goal.

*Almost Paradise* was a part of that plan. The original reason he'd accepted the job on the boat was to keep an eye on Kenzie. He'd enjoyed the job, but now more than ever he definitely wanted to be close to Kenzie in case anything else happened.

Tom Banks, one of the fishing captains he worked with on occasion, strode across the docks toward him. "Hey, there. You staying on *Almost Paradise* tonight?"

Jimmy James shook his head. "Not yet. Tomorrow, we'll get the boat all cleaned up, and then the next day we'll leave with our guests."

He glanced at the yacht in the distance. "Who's staying on it now?"

"No one. Why?"

Tom let out a surprised grunt as he narrowed his eyes. "I thought for sure I saw someone onboard about twenty minutes ago."

# CHAPTER TWELVE

CAUTIOUSLY, Jimmy James boarded *Almost Paradise* and walked the perimeter of the deck. His muscles felt tense as adrenaline pumped through him. At the first sign of trouble, he would act.

Nobody was supposed to be on this boat. He couldn't imagine why someone might have been . . . unless it had something to do with Kenzie's attack.

That's what he intended on figuring out.

He pulled up the flashlight on his phone and shone it around. He didn't think anybody was still onboard, but he wanted to take them by surprise if they were.

As he reached the main salon, he jiggled the door. It was locked. Good. This whole boat should be locked up.

He pulled out his key, unlocked the door, and paced inside, shining his light around the room.

Everything appeared to be in place. The teak floor looked clean. The pillows on the beige couches were in place. The TV still hung on the wall. The room even smelled like a mix of lemony furniture polish, saltwater, and soft leather.

He continued through the main deck, searching the game room, meeting room, and dining area.

He then did the same throughout the next two levels and the bridge.

But nothing was out of place, and no one was hiding behind any corners or furniture.

So, what had Tom seen? Had someone else really been on the boat?

Jimmy James' gut told him this had something to do with what happened to Kenzie.

The question was what?

---

KENZIE RELEASED a deep breath as she waited on the deck of Cassidy and Ty's place the next morning. Jimmy James was supposed to arrive at any moment to pick her up and take her to the docks.

To pass time, Kenzie sat on the swing tucked on

the far side of the deck and used her foot to push herself back and forth. As she did, her thoughts tumbled inside her.

Nightmares had plagued her all night. She'd awakened in the night, her bed feeling as if it swayed with the water. Terror had consumed her as she wondered if she'd regained consciousness only to discover she was in the middle of the ocean again.

Instead, she'd been safe in her bed at Ty and Cassidy's house.

Thank goodness.

As sunlight filled the sky, she'd stared at her phone, wondering if she should call her father. She planned to. But she hadn't. Not yet.

Maybe she needed more time to pull herself together before they talked.

The swing continued to pendulate back and forth as she debated.

Kenzie had been through a lot in the past month since she took the job aboard *Almost Paradise*. But nothing had shaken her up as much as what had happened yesterday. She'd be foolish to think she could just bounce back after her ordeal and continue on with life as normal.

But she also felt as if she had no choice. She

wasn't going to let someone scare her away from doing what she wanted to do.

Maybe time was the only thing that would help dispel her anxiety.

Finally, she spotted Jimmy James' truck coming down the lane cutting between the marsh grass in front of the cottage. She grabbed her suitcase and headed down the steps to meet him.

With the truck still running, Jimmy James climbed out to meet her. Just as her feet hit the driveway, he pulled her into a long hug, giving every indication he didn't want to let go.

"Good morning," he whispered in her ear.

The affection in his voice nearly took Kenzie's breath away. "Good morning."

"Did you sleep okay last night?" He kept his arms around her waist, pulling away just enough to see her face.

Kenzie nodded, not bothering to tell him about the nightmares she'd had. "As well as can be expected."

His lips set in a grim line as if he guessed how difficult the night had been. He pointed at her suitcase. "You're still on for the trip?"

"Nothing could keep me away." When Kenzie realized just how literally she meant the words, she frowned again. Not even her life being on the line was going to change her mind.

He stepped back and squeezed her hand before grabbing her suitcase. "Let's get down to the boat then. The crew should be meeting us in another hour."

"Let's go." Kenzie climbed in the truck.

They were only about fifteen minutes away from the marina. But the ride was mostly quiet. Jimmy James didn't push her to talk, and she appreciated that fact.

Finally, they pulled up to the docks. But before she climbed from the truck, her phone buzzed. She looked down and saw she'd gotten a text message.

The words there made her eyes widen.

DON'T MAKE **us warn you again.**

## CHAPTER THIRTEEN

AS JIMMY JAMES remained in his truck, he stared at the text on Kenzie's phone and shook his head. "I can't believe someone sent this to you."

Kenzie rubbed her arms, her eyes losing some of the light they'd contained this morning. "It says *us*. That implies there's more than one person involved. But this whole thing just doesn't make sense to me. It doesn't matter how I look at what happened, I don't know who would do this to me or why."

She pressed her lips together and stared out the window as she trembled with barely contained emotions.

"You don't think . . ." Jimmy James couldn't bring himself to finish the statement. But the theory that had formed in his mind last night wouldn't leave his thoughts.

She glanced over at him, her eyes inquisitive. "Think what?"

"It's nothing. Just a crazy idea." He waved a hand, trying to brush off the thought. He shouldn't have started to say anything. He already knew this conversation wasn't going to turn out well.

"I want to know. What are you thinking?"

Jimmy James let out a long breath, wishing it wasn't too late to go back. "You don't think . . . that your dad would . . . try to scare you off from working this job by doing something like this, do you?"

Kenzie's eyes widened as if his words had truly shocked her. "What? No. No way. Why would you even suggest that?"

"He's the only person I can think of who has a motive to keep you away. He doesn't want you doing this job."

She continued to shake her head, an incredulous look in her eyes. "But I could have been *killed*. My dad would never put me in that situation."

"I agree that he wouldn't." Jimmy James shifted, carefully trying to find the right words. "It's just that whoever set you adrift in the ocean left you with the phone and . . ."

Kenzie crossed her arms and raised her chin, making it clear she didn't want to explore his theory any longer. "It wasn't my dad. That's one theory I'm going to have to nix right away."

Jimmy James raised his hands, trying to calm the situation before it spun out of control. "I'm sorry. I shouldn't have even suggested it."

Her shoulders slumped as she ran a hand through her hair. "It's okay. You're right—we do need to examine every angle here, even the ones that I don't like. It's just that my father . . ."

"I understand. Mentioning him is off limits." Jimmy James stared at Kenzie another moment, hating how heavy everything felt right now.

When would the two of them catch a break? It didn't appear that would be happening anytime soon.

"Are you ready?" He nodded toward *Almost Paradise* in the distance. He could see some of the crew had already gathered on the dock.

"Looks like they're a little early too. Let's go."

They grabbed their luggage and started across the docks. As Jimmy James glanced at the crew, he noticed someone new standing with them—a twenty-something woman with short dark hair. The woman had olive skin, a line of piercings up the side of her ear, and tattoos playing peekaboo from beneath her shirt sleeve.

She talked with the crew as if she were one of them.

Tension mounted between his shoulders as he sensed something was off.

Kenzie leaned closer and lowered her voice. "Do you know who that is?"

"No." Jimmy James' jaw twitched. "Let's find out."

---

"YOU MUST BE CAPTAIN GAMBLE." The woman extended her hand, her long red fingernails making a stark statement against the weathered marina behind her. "My name is Araminta, Araminta Linton."

Kenzie watched as Jimmy James shook her outstretched hand. "Nice to meet you, Araminta. I take it you know the rest of the crew?"

"We've worked together before," Araminta purred. "That's why I'm thrilled to be here now."

Jimmy James shifted, a knot forming on his brow. "What do you mean?"

Araminta blinked as she stared at them, a mix of

confusion and satisfaction in her gaze. "You mean, you don't know?"

"Know what?" A touch of irritation grew in his voice. "What's going on here? Someone needs to start explaining."

"I'm sorry." She put a hand over her heart, even though the apology looked too overblown to be sincere. "I thought Mr. Robertson told you. He hired me to be the second stew."

Alarm raced through Kenzie. She couldn't have just heard the woman correctly . . . "I'm the second stew."

Araminta raised her hands defensively, her gold bracelets clattered down her arms. "Look, I don't know what's going on here. I'm not trying to start trouble. I'm just telling you that Mr. Robertson called me and asked me if I would be willing to work this charter."

"He should have run that past me first." Jimmy James' gaze darkened. "Especially since I'm the captain."

"I'm sorry." Araminta frowned. "I feel like I've made everything awkward, and I didn't mean to do that. I just showed up here to do a job."

Jimmy James let out a puff of air before running

a hand over his jaw. "Let me call Mr. Robertson and find out what's going on. In the meantime, stay put."

Kenzie's stomach squeezed tighter.

Had she just been demoted? What sense did that make?

She didn't know what was going on here, but whatever it was she didn't like it.

And if Kenzie were honest with herself . . . she didn't exactly like the new stew either, especially not when she saw the way the woman looked at Jimmy James.

# CHAPTER FOURTEEN

JIMMY JAMES WALKED from the crew toward the marina office. As he did, he dialed Mr. Robertson's number.

The man picked up on the fourth ring. "Captain Gamble. I was just about to call you."

Jimmy James' jaw flexed as he paused in the shade near the front door and turned to stare out at the marina. "I hear we have a new stew."

"After everything that happened yesterday, I wasn't sure if Ms. Anderson would be joining us or not. To be on the safe side, I decided to hire another stew."

Jimmy James had talked to Mr. Robertson and told him what was going on. But he hadn't mentioned anything about hiring someone else.

"Don't you think you should have talked to me about that first?" Jimmy James gripped the phone so hard that his knuckles ached.

"I didn't mean to step on your toes. I was just trying to help out."

"The captain usually chooses his crew. You know that." Jimmy James couldn't let this slide. If he didn't create firm boundaries, he'd be walked all over—and that was no way to lead a boat. The original crew was already in place when he got this job. But any new members? He expected to have a say-so.

"I understand that's the way things generally work. But you and I both have to admit the circumstances were anything but normal."

Jimmy James couldn't argue with that. He wasn't supposed to captain *Almost Paradise*, but the first captain had died and the second had come down with a stomach bug. Jimmy James had practically gotten this job by default.

"Look, I can attest to Araminta's skills," Mr. Robertson continued. "She's an excellent stew, and I think she'll do a wonderful job on the boat. She'll be an asset. I promise."

Jimmy James continued to stare at the marina around him, keeping one eye open for any signs of trouble. "Still, you should have run this by me first. How do you think Kenzie feels right now?"

"She can still be second stew if that helps, although she *is* the one with the least amount of experience. It will be good to have somebody else onboard to help carry the load, don't you think?"

Jimmy James stared at the crew in the distance. He didn't like adding another stranger to the mix, especially not this late in the game.

And especially not with everything that had happened.

But Mr. Robertson was correct. *Almost Paradise* was his boat, and he could call the shots as he pleased.

Which was one more reason why Jimmy James wanted his own boat for charters.

After speaking his piece, he ended the call and started back toward the group.

Jimmy James prayed he would have one charter that went without a hitch.

————————

AS KENZIE WORKED to get the guest staterooms ready, she couldn't help but notice the instant bond that Sunni Briggs, the chief stew, and Araminta seem to have.

She wasn't jealous. She really wasn't. But, in her experience, whenever three women were together, one was always the odd person out.

Even with some of her best friends that had still been the case.

Kenzie let out a sigh and tucked the sheets beneath the mattress, smoothing out any wrinkles. That was fine. She wasn't working on this yacht to make friends.

But she and Sunni had come a long way since their very first charter together when the woman acted like she couldn't stand her. Kenzie thought the two of them were making progress, but that didn't seem to be the case right now.

Just then, Sunni stepped into the master stateroom and paused. She pushed her honey blonde hair over her shoulder as she stood in front of Kenzie, her sturdy frame standing at full height.

"Kenzie . . . I was hoping to catch you," she started. "I've been thinking things through, and I think you should be third stew."

Kenzie smoothed out one last wrinkle on the bed before straightening and staring at Sunni. "You're demoting me?"

"Don't say it like that." Sunni tilted her head to the side, and something about the way her gaze flickered made it appear she wanted to roll her eyes but stopped herself. "It's just that Araminta has been doing this kind of work for four years. This is your first season working on a yacht of this size, and I really think we could benefit from Araminta's experience."

Kenzie wasn't ready to concede that easily. "But I've done a good job. I've done nothing but help you."

Sunni shrugged. "I don't know what to say. It's not personal. But my decision has been made. I just wanted to let you know."

Kenzie stared at Sunni for another moment before shaking her head. Arguing would get her nowhere as it appeared Sunni's mind was already made up. Plus, it was her choice as chief stew.

"I understand," Kenzie finally said. "But for the record, I still don't agree with the decision."

"Hey, you two!" Araminta appeared, a grin on her face. "Listen, I have a question for you. Do either of you know if Captain Gamble is single?"

Kenzie's breath caught. She and Jimmy James had agreed to keep their relationship under wraps. But . . .

"I don't know." Sunni's eyes flashed as she turned toward Kenzie. "Is Captain Gamble single, Kenzie?"

Her cheeks burned. "It doesn't matter. The captain's not going to date a crew member."

Araminta's eyebrows flickered up. "We'll see about that . . . he's so hot. He has this bad boy vibe that always gets me."

Kenzie felt Sunni's scrutinizing gaze on her. But Kenzie refused to give Sunni any clue as to how she felt.

Instead, she turned to head into the bathroom and get it ready. When she glanced back, Sunni and Araminta were both gone.

Kenzie let out a sigh, fighting irritation.

She supposed she had bigger worries.

She remembered the messages she'd gotten. *Go home. Don't make us warn you again.*

Whoever had set her adrift wasn't done with her yet. Apparently, they didn't want her working on the boat. But she was perplexed as to why.

Jimmy James' theory still caused a surge of defensiveness. Sure, her father was adamantly opposed to her taking this direction for her future and forgoing med school. But he'd never put her in harm's way. She knew him well enough to know that.

It just didn't make sense that anyone else would want to get rid of her that badly.

Kenzie let out a sigh as she continued to work.

She could turn these thoughts over in her mind all day. But that wasn't going to lead to any answers. For now, the best thing she could do was to concentrate on her work.

And try also to forget about the fact that she was now the third stew.

# CHAPTER FIFTEEN

AS THE CREW busied themselves getting the boat ready for their guests to arrive tomorrow morning, Jimmy James wandered into the marina office looking for Stevie-o.

Jimmy James found him sitting at his desk.

The man glanced up and rubbed his shaggy beard. "Jimmy James. What brings you down here? Don't you have a charter to get ready for?"

Jimmy James paused on the other side of his desk. "I do. I just wanted to ask you a question."

Stevie-o crossed his arms and leaned back. "What do you need to know?"

"The police are trying to figure out where Kenzie's captors launched their boat. I know they've talked to you, but I wanted to find out some information myself. Did you see anything unusual happening at the marina on the night Kenzie was abducted?"

Stevie-o let out a tight breath before shaking his head. "I wish I could help you. But I can't. I didn't see anything."

"No one suspicious was hanging here at the harbor?"

"You were always the one who had an eye for trouble. Not me. I just like to make sure everyone plays by the rules and pays me on time."

"What about the security cameras you were going to put in after that last incident here? Did you ever do that?" Jimmy James hadn't seen them—and he would have noticed—but he wanted to ask anyway.

Stevie-o shook his head. "No. I don't have the funding yet. They're still on the agenda, however."

Tension remained between Jimmy James' shoulders. This whole meeting had proven unsuccessful. He knew no more now than he did when he came here.

As he started to leave, Stevie-o called his name, and Jimmy James paused.

"There *is* one thing that you might want to

know." Stevie-o's cheek twitched as if he was about to share bad news.

"What's that?"

"I thought you should know that someone is trying to buy this place." He swung his head around to indicate he was talking about the marina. "And I might just take him up on his offer."

"What?" Jimmy James didn't bother to hide the surprise from his voice.

Stevie-o shrugged. "The offer came in a few days ago, and I've been entertaining the idea."

Jimmy James stepped closer, not wanting to leave without more information. "Who's trying to buy the marina?"

"A man named Murphy Bassett. I don't know too much about him except that he has enough money to pay cash. His offer might solve all the financial problems I've been struggling with."

Jimmy James let out a grunt. He knew all about Stevie-o's financial issues.

What he didn't know was what to think about this bit of news. His first reaction was to rebel against the idea. Then again, change had never been his favorite thing. He and Stevie-o didn't always see eye to eye, but at least Jimmy James knew what to expect from the man.

He glanced at his watch. "I've got to get back."

Stevie-o nodded. "I hope you find whoever did this to Kenzie."

So did Jimmy James.

---

AFTER THE CREW FINISHED CLEANING, which took almost the entire day, they met in the salon for a preference sheet meeting.

Jimmy James handed out printed information on each of their incoming guests.

Kenzie stared at the papers, studying the profiles.

The primary guest was Edgar Abernathy, a man who'd founded a high-end chain of jewelry stores known as Abernathy's. Apparently, the stores had more than one hundred fifty locations throughout the US.

The picture of the man showed he was in his sixties with salt-and-pepper hair and an unnatural-looking tan. His thick hair, along with his perfect white teeth, gave off an air of affluence, and his smile screamed self-importance.

He was married to Roselyn, who was in her forties and beautiful, with long, blonde hair and a trim body.

Roman Abernathy, Edgar's son from his first marriage, would also be joining them. He was twenty-five years old and liked playing water polo as well as tennis.

Roselyn's best friend, Tiffany, would be there along with Woodrow, Edgar's brother.

The guests were headed to a jewelry trade show in St. Augustine, Florida. They'd chartered a one-way trip, wanting to arrive at the destination in style.

Kenzie already had an inkling as to what these people would be like, and she had to brace herself for what some of their requests might be. The wealthier the guests, the more they liked to be waited on hand and foot, it seemed.

On the way down, they'd stop at a couple of ports, but the entire trip would be done in only a few days.

It seemed easy enough.

When they finished their meeting, Jimmy James announced that the crew had the rest of the evening off to enjoy before their charter began. Kenzie looked at her watch and saw it was 6:00 p.m.

"Do you want to grab something and eat at the beach?" Jimmy James' voice pulled her out of her introspection.

She glanced back and saw him standing behind

her. She offered a grateful smile before saying, "That sounds great."

"Just let me grab a few things, and we can be on our way."

A few minutes later, they left the boat and started across the marina.

As they walked past the office, Kenzie froze. She scanned everything around her, searching for the source of her subtle, distressed feeling.

"Kenzie?" Jimmy James paused and turned toward her.

She didn't dare tear her eyes away from her surroundings.

Somebody was watching her.

She was certain of it.

Kenzie sucked in a breath when she spotted a man standing beside a motorcycle in the parking lot.

She grabbed Jimmy James' arm and nodded at the stranger, who quickly put his camera away. "He's taking pictures of me."

"What?" Jimmy James' muscles bristled.

The next instant, he took off in a run, clearly determined to catch the man.

# CHAPTER SIXTEEN

JIMMY JAMES TORE across the parking lot, intending to grab the man taking pictures of Kenzie.

Before Jimmy James reached him, the man revved his motorcycle engine. He cast one more glance over his shoulder before zooming away.

Jimmy James knew by the time he climbed in his truck and took off after the guy that it would be too late.

As he watched the man zip away from the marina, Jimmy James grabbed his phone to call in the motorcycle's license plate number to Chief Chambers. She promised to run the plates and to alert her officers to keep their eyes open for the motorcycle.

Wasting no more time, he jogged back toward

Kenzie. He spotted her leaning against the marina office. He paused when he reached her, noting with relief that she was okay.

"The man got away," he told her. "But I called Chief Chambers and told her what happened. I also gave her the license number, and she's going to look into it. Are you okay?"

Kenzie nodded, even though she still looked dazed with her wide eyes and trembling limbs. "Everything's just shaken me up. I don't seem to have time to catch my breath before something else hits me."

"I know." He lowered his voice. "I know, and I'm so sorry."

He wanted to pull her into his arms again and tell her that everything would be okay. But that wasn't the best choice. If the rest of the crew knew the two of them were dating, that could cause issues on their next charter. The last thing they needed was to stir up more trouble on *Almost Paradise*. The boat had more than its fair share already.

Even though part of Jimmy James wanted to shout from the rooftops how honored he was that someone like Kenzie had fallen for someone like him, he knew it was better to keep things between the two of them under wraps.

"Hopefully, we'll hear something from Chief Chambers soon," Jimmy James finally told Kenzie. "You didn't recognize that guy, did you?"

Kenzie shook her head, her arms pulled tight over her chest. "He was too far away, but from what I could tell, he didn't look familiar."

Jimmy James stared at her another moment, concerned by everything she'd been through. How many burdens could a person bear before they broke?

Maybe the best thing right now would be to get Kenzie away from this marina. This place seemed to be the source of most of her troubles.

As they stepped toward his truck, a BMW zoomed into the lot, the driver going entirely too fast. Jimmy James bristled at the driver's carelessness. The next instant, the door opened, and a short, wiry man wearing a button-up shirt and khakis stepped out. A cocky grin stretched across his face.

Before Jimmy James could give the guy a piece of his mind, the man hurried toward them, his words as brisk as his steps. "Good evening. I'm Murphy Bassett. Have any of you seen Stevie-o Peters?"

Jimmy James' breath caught.

*This* was Murphy Bassett? The man trying to buy this marina?

Why would an uppity man like him want to buy a rundown place like this? In Jimmy James' experience, people like Murphy Bassett preferred upscale places that would serve as another trophy on their shelf of accomplishments. They didn't like working-man's marinas.

Another thing that didn't make sense.

And Jimmy James didn't like it when things didn't make sense.

———

"STEVIE-O IS PROBABLY IN THE OFFICE." Kenzie nodded toward the marina's front entrance, surprised that Jimmy James hadn't spoken up yet. Instead, he almost seemed to be sizing this man up.

"Fantastic." Murphy offered an enthusiastic nod before glancing around. "This place has a lot of potential, don't you think?"

She continued to eye the man suspiciously. Who was this guy? And why did Jimmy James seem so tense beside her? Did he know the man?

Clearly, there was more to this story.

Kenzie raised her chin. "I think the marina is perfect as it is. It has character."

The man let out a hearty chuckle. "Character? Is

that a nice way of saying it's a dump? But if the right person put the money into it . . ." He winked and grinned again.

Something about the man seemed slimy. Kenzie couldn't put her finger on what, but she already didn't trust him.

"You two have a nice evening," Murphy said before entering the building.

Before Kenzie could get Jimmy James' reaction to the man, Eddie—the first mate—strode from his car toward them. His lanky frame swung with every step and his short haircut almost made him look like a sailor.

"Who was that?" He nodded toward the door to the marina office.

"Murphy Bassett." Jimmy James' jaw tightened, and his scowl deepened as he said the man's name.

"Should I know who that is?" Eddie raised his eyebrows.

"He wants to buy this marina," Jimmy James said.

Kenzie gasped, uncertain if she'd heard him correctly. "What? I didn't even know this place was for sale."

"It's not. But apparently that guy made a really

good offer that Stevie-o is having a hard time refusing."

"By the sound of it, he wants to fix this place up. But I wonder what exactly that means." It wouldn't surprise Kenzie if this guy wanted to completely renovate this marina until the area was unrecognizable.

Eddie glanced around. "Fixing this place up doesn't sound like a bad idea."

"If it was just replacing some of the docks and updating the marina office, that would be one thing. But something tells me that that man has bigger plans." Jimmy James' gaze darkened as he stared in the distance. "It could devastate this area."

"What do you mean?" Kenzie knew she wasn't fully grasping the scope of his statement.

"If this place becomes more of a luxury marina than a workingman's marina, that guy will inflate what he charges people for boat slips. So many of the fishermen here can barely make ends meet. A price increase like that . . . it could take them out of business."

A bad feeling grew in Kenzie's stomach.

This was just one more thing she needed to try not to worry about.

But something just didn't rest well in her gut.

## CHAPTER SEVENTEEN

JIMMY JAMES and Kenzie grabbed some fish and chips from a local restaurant and then took their meals to the beach. He laid out a blanket, and they sat watching the ocean waves roll in.

He wasn't sure if the sight would bring Kenzie comfort or not after her ordeal, but she didn't seem to mind. Plus, spending one-on-one time together away from the crew was nice.

*Any* time he could spend around Kenzie was nice.

As they ate, Jimmy James told stories of going fishing with his dad on the beach, learning to operate a boat at only eight years old, and shucking oysters to earn extra money as a preteen.

In return, Kenzie told him about playing volleyball for her high school team, how her dad had shown her how to suture a cut while in middle school, and how he'd tested her on what organs of the body served what function as part of casual dinner conversation.

When they finished eating, Jimmy James turned to her. He had something on his mind that he couldn't delay sharing any more. "Part of me wishes we weren't going on that charter."

Kenzie glanced up at him, that sweet, innocent look in her eyes. "Why is that?"

"Because then I could spend time here at the beach kissing you."

"That actually doesn't sound too bad." She grinned before reaching up and pressing her lips against his.

Jimmy James wanted to lean into it more, to let himself get lost in the moment. Instead, he lingered close to her, inexplicitly drawn to the woman. Even when he'd dated before, he'd never felt this level of attraction . . . even though he knew that it went deeper than a mere crush.

"It doesn't sound bad, does it?" Jimmy James murmured. "But we probably need to keep this thing between us quiet—at least for this charter."

The wind blew Kenzie's hair away from her face

while the fading sunlight illuminated her gentle profile. "I agree. Sunni is already acting like she has a chip on her shoulder toward me again. I thought we were past that, but I guess not. I don't need to give the crew any more ammunition not to like me."

"No, you don't. But I don't like hearing that she's treating you poorly."

"Girls can be mean, and some women are just girls who've gotten a little older. Some do a better job of hiding their insecurities than others."

"When did you get to be so wise?"

Kenzie pushed a lock of hair behind her ear. "That depends on who you ask. Some people don't think I'm all that wise."

"Then they're wrong. I think you're brilliant."

She gave him a playful side-glance. "Now you're just trying to flatter me."

"Except I'm not. I mean it. You are the total package, Kenzie Anderson."

She raised her head to him. Instead of saying anything, she pressed her lips into his.

And Jimmy James wasn't complaining.

THE CLASHING EMOTIONS inside Kenzie made her feel unbalanced as she and Jimmy James headed back to the harbor.

One moment, she felt on top of the world because of the new developments between her and Jimmy James. Warmth filled her chest every time she thought about him.

The next moment, she remembered how she'd almost died. She remembered the man she'd seen taking pictures of her. Somehow, she knew her troubles weren't over.

As they rode back, she squeezed Jimmy James' hand. Quiet settled between them. She liked that Jimmy James didn't always need to fill the void with conversation. Sometimes quiet said much more.

By the time they arrived at the marina, the sun had sunk below the horizon, and a few wispy gray clouds lingered in the fading remnants of light.

Kenzie felt reluctant for this evening to end. She knew several days would most likely pass without very many meaningful conversations taking place between her and Jimmy James. Sure, they might be able to steal a few minutes alone here and there. But nothing like what she'd experienced over the last two days.

She'd never fallen in love before, but this must be what the start of it felt like.

Slowly, they walked back to *Almost Paradise*.

Before they reached the boat, Jimmy James pulled her out of sight behind the marina office. "You know that if you need anything while you're on the boat—"

"That you'll be there," she finished with a smile. "Yes, I know. Thank you."

He stared at her, worry staining his gaze. "I'm still hopeful that we'll hear something from Chief Chambers tonight about that motorcycle."

"Me too. I'm glad you got the license number."

They stared at each other another moment, and Kenzie hoped he might kiss her one more time.

But before he could, a roar in the distance caught her ear.

They both swung their heads toward the noise.

Kenzie sucked in a breath.

A smaller fishing boat on the other end of the marina was on fire.

And someone aboard screamed for help.

# CHAPTER EIGHTEEN

"STAY HERE AND CALL 911!" Jimmy James started toward the scene. "I've got to go help."

"Got it." Kenzie's hands trembled as she pulled her phone out.

She wished she could do something, but she wasn't sure what. The first thing would be calling 911.

Her voice sounded shaky as she explained to the operator what was happening. The dispatcher promised help was on the way. Thankfully, the island was small, so hopefully it wouldn't take long.

Kenzie remained grounded another moment, not wanting to get in the way. Instead, she closed her eyes and lifted a prayer that everyone would be protected. The person in the boat. Jimmy James.

What happened? How had the boat caught fire?

Was it an accident? Or had this somehow happened on purpose?

She couldn't stay here, she realized. She'd gone through two years of med school. If the person she'd heard scream needed help, she could offer some initial assistance. She couldn't let her fears or trauma hold her back.

She started toward the scene when she heard something crack behind her.

As she froze, a hand went over her mouth. An arm wrapped around her midsection, holding her in place.

Then a gravelly voice said in her ear, "All you had to do was listen."

JIMMY JAMES SPRINTED toward the fire.

The flames continued to grow higher and stronger with every second.

Another shout sounded.

He narrowed his eyes. Was that a man waving his hands aboard the burning boat?

His heart hammered harder into his chest.

It was.

Jimmy James rushed down the dock toward the

small fishing vessel. Fire licked around him as smoke billowed in the air.

As soon as the flames reached the fuel tank . . . things would get even uglier. His throat tightened at the thought.

An older man was trapped on the boat. He seemed unable to move as he stared at Jimmy James, his eyes wide with fear.

Jimmy James paused at the edge of the dock. Flames separated him from the man. Heat from the blaze made his skin feel like it was burning.

The man waved his hands in the air. "Help me!"

"Jump in the water!" Jimmy James shouted. It was the only solution that made sense. Otherwise, the flames would reach the man at any moment.

The man glanced beside him, and his face turned ashen. The tendon on his neck showed a visible pulse. "What if I can't get back out of the water?"

"I'll help you. You've got to do it now—the fire is about to reach the fuel tank!"

The man's eyes widened. As another burst flared to life, he dove into the water.

Jimmy James ran to the edge of the dock and lay on his stomach. He reached his hand toward the man, who swam through the dark water toward him.

But the fire inched closer and closer. The flames could claim this dry, rickety dock at any minute. His heart pounded harder.

Finally, the man was close enough that Jimmy James could reach down and grab his arms. After a few heaves, he managed to pull the man onto the dock.

He kept a hand on the man's arm and led him away from the inflamed boat slip. He didn't stop running until they were in the parking lot.

Just as they reached that area, an explosion sounded.

Jimmy James shielded the man as debris rained down on them.

He glanced around for an extinguisher. But one of those wouldn't begin to touch a fire of this size.

He prayed the worst of it was over. And it probably was—unless the fire reached another boat or the dock. Hopefully, fire and rescue would arrive before that.

He turned to the man. "Are you okay?"

The man nodded as he coughed, and water dripped from his hair.

Sirens sounded in the distance. Help was on the way.

His shoulders sagged with relief.

How had this blaze even started? Firefighters would have to figure that out.

Jimmy James glanced back, searching for Kenzie. But he didn't see her lingering anywhere close.

Maybe she went inside the marina office.

He turned back to the man he'd rescued. "Will you be okay here by yourself for a moment?"

The man nodded, and Jimmy James helped him to a seat outside the marina office. A quick glance inside showed she wasn't there.

As Jimmy James strode away, he continued scanning the area for Kenzie.

He still didn't see her.

He picked up his pace, feeling an intuitive sense of urgency.

Behind him, the rescue crew pulled onto the scene. Firefighters jumped from their trucks with their hoses.

Good. At least Jimmy James knew the fire was being handled.

But the bad feeling in his gut continued to grow. He still didn't see Kenzie.

Urgency gripped him.

He rushed to the backside of the marina office, to the area where he'd left her.

Only an old propane tank and trash cans waited there.

He paced a few more steps toward the corner, just to be sure he hadn't missed anything.

That's when he saw a man in black dragging Kenzie toward the woods. Her eyes were wide with a fear visible even in the dim light.

"Hey!" Jimmy James shouted.

The man's gaze turned to him.

Jimmy James braced himself for whatever was about to happen next.

## CHAPTER NINETEEN

KENZIE HEARD the man's breath catch. He froze and seemed to stare at Jimmy James. Then he shifted as if looking in the other direction.

She saw the police vehicles pulling onto the scene, their sirens blaring and lights flashing.

The next instant, the man shoved her forward and took off in a run.

She tumbled to the ground, her palms and knees scraping against the gravel. The breath left her lungs as she tensed, wondering what might happen next. Shock continued to course through her.

Jimmy James dashed toward her and knelt at her side. "Kenzie . . . are you okay?"

She nodded, determined to reassure him. But

her limbs were trembling again, giving away her inner turmoil. "I'm fine."

"Did that man hurt you?"

"No, I'm fine. Really. Go after him. Catch him."

He stared at her another moment before nodding and racing after the man.

As he did, Kenzie rose to full height, wiping her palms against her legs. She watched Jimmy James as he disappeared into the woods where the man had gone.

She prayed he'd be able to catch the guy. If they could interrogate that man, a lot of their questions would be answered. Maybe she could put her mind at ease. But the last thing she wanted was for Jimmy James to get hurt.

As he disappeared from sight, she glanced in the other direction. Fire crews were already putting out the flames. They had spread to two other boats and destroyed part of the dock.

Had anyone been injured? She hoped that hadn't been the case.

What was going on at this marina? Why were so many bad things happening?

Kenzie remained where she was. She kept waiting, hoping to see Jimmy James appear, dragging out the man who'd grabbed her.

But there were no signs of movement in the woods.

She nibbled on her bottom lip as she tried to figure out what to do.

Track down Cassidy and tell her what had happened?

Run after Jimmy James herself?

Kenzie wasn't sure. But she couldn't just stand here and do nothing . . . especially not if Jimmy James could potentially be hurt.

———

JIMMY JAMES PAUSED in the woods and glanced around.

Where had the man gone? He couldn't have just disappeared.

But Jimmy James didn't hear any footsteps.

That left only one possibility.

This guy could be hiding, waiting to attack.

Jimmy James took each step slowly as he glanced around, looking for any sign of where the guy had gone.

But darkness filled the air, and it was almost impossible to see anything in the thick maritime forest.

His muscles bristled with every step as he braced himself for potential trouble.

In the distance, he heard the fire engines. Heard their sirens. Heard the firefighters working to put out the flames.

Water bordered one side of these woods, along with the marina and a road. Eventually, the wooded lot ended at a stretch of houses on the far side of the property.

Jimmy James hoped this guy hadn't gone toward the houses. Hoped he wouldn't put anybody else in danger.

But without knowing any more about their suspect, Jimmy James didn't know what to expect.

He skirted around an oak tree, still on guard.

Just as he stepped beyond it, a stick snapped behind him.

He turned to see where the sound came from.

But before he could see anything, something hard came down on his head and everything went black.

# CHAPTER TWENTY

KENZIE STEPPED CLOSER to the woods. She shouldn't do this. It wasn't what Jimmy James would want.

But the police were occupied with the fire. No one else was around. Every minute counted right now.

*What are you going to do if you find him? You have no weapon and you're not strong enough to defend him against an attacker.*

Kenzie shoved her apprehension aside.

Instead, she stepped into the woods. As her foot hit a thick branch that had fallen on the ground, she reached down and grabbed it. Bouncing it in her hands, it felt solid but not too heavy. She might need this.

She held it like a baseball bat on her shoulder as she quietly walked through the woods, listening for any signs as to where Jimmy James might have gone.

Worst-case scenarios tried to pummel her, but she pushed them back. Kenzie couldn't let fear win right now. Jimmy James had put himself at risk uncountable times for her. Now she needed to do the same for him.

Her stomach clenched with each step deeper she traveled into the woods. The shadows were dark here under the canopy of trees.

There were so many places a person could hide, could be waiting to pounce . . .

Chills raced up her arms.

She wanted to call Jimmy James' name, but she didn't dare give away her presence.

Still, why didn't she hear him? See him?

He could have gone to the road and run that way. But Kenzie didn't think that was the case. She'd watched the road before she entered the woods. She hadn't seen any activity there.

As she took another step, she nearly tumbled over something.

She looked down and gasped. "Jimmy James?"

He lay unmoving, his body nearly concealed by the thick underbrush.

Was he dead?

"Jimmy James?" she repeated as she leaned down to shake him.

At once, he groaned and tried to sit up.

He was alive!

*Thank You, Jesus!*

But what had happened?

---

"KENZIE?" Jimmy James muttered. He blinked, wondering if he was seeing things. Was that really Kenzie's beautiful face staring down at him?

She cradled his head in her lap. "Oh, my goodness. Are you okay? What happened?"

He rubbed his throbbing head. "I'm okay."

"You don't look like you're okay. Who did this to you? Where did he go?"

"He must have run off. I didn't see his face."

"Let's get you up." Kenzie rose, put her arm around his waist, and attempted to help him to his feet.

He forced himself to stand, despite the pounding in his head. Just as he found his balance, another thought hit him.

He turned to Kenzie. "What are you doing out here?"

"I had to come find you."

Alarm raced through him until his back went ramrod straight. "That wasn't smart. I appreciate that you want to help me, but what if this guy had confronted you again? What if he'd grabbed you and taken you away?"

Her lip tugged down in a frown. "He didn't. I'm fine. I had to know that you were okay."

Tension stretched across his chest. He wanted to argue more, but he didn't. What was done was done.

Still, Kenzie coming out here hadn't been a good idea. He wouldn't be able to forgive himself if something happened to her because of him.

She helped him through the woods, back to the marina.

As soon as they cleared the tree line, his gaze found the docks and he saw that the flames had been extinguished. Rotating red and blue lights filled the air. The gritty smell of smoke still lingered like a thick fog.

Jimmy James let out a deep breath. Certain areas of his life felt like they were on repeat . . . especially when it came to talking to Chief Chambers.

Kenzie frowned beside him and kept her arm around him as they walked toward the police cars in the distance.

## CHAPTER TWENTY-ONE

KENZIE STOOD with Cassidy and Jimmy James on the docks as firefighters examined the charred boats.

The police chief had taken one look at Jimmy James and motioned for a medic to come over. But Jimmy James shooed the man away, insisting he was okay. The medic made one more attempt before shrugging at Cassidy and giving up.

Instead, Cassidy took their statements, her concerned gaze traveling from them back to the remains of the marina fire. "Trouble certainly seems to be following you."

Kenzie frowned and nodded, knowing she couldn't deny the statement. "I know. It's like I have a target on my back."

"You didn't catch a glimpse of this guy's face?" Cassidy clarified.

Her mind raced back in time, but everything was a blur. It had been so dark and . . . "No, I wish I did. But it was too dark, and I didn't see anything."

Jimmy James stepped closer to Kenzie, almost as if he feared letting her out of arm's reach would put her in danger again. "I didn't either."

Cassidy tapped her pencil against her lips in thought. "I almost wonder if that fire was set just to get you away from Kenzie."

Kenzie drew in a breath at the chief's theory. "What? It was on purpose?"

"That's right. Wilson—the man Jimmy James rescued—apparently fell asleep on his boat. When he woke up, he smelled gasoline. He saw someone in black light a match, and the next thing he knew everything was on fire."

"I can't believe someone did this on purpose." Jimmy James' eyes narrowed.

"I'm beginning to believe nothing will surprise me anymore." Cassidy studied Jimmy James one more time. "Are you sure you don't need to go to the clinic?"

"I'm fine," he insisted.

"Are you sure?"

"I'm positive."

An officer called to Cassidy, and she turned back to Kenzie and Jimmy James. "I'll talk to you guys again in a bit."

"We'll be here," Jimmy James said.

Kenzie drew in a deep breath, reality still not fully hitting her.

Before she could talk things over with Jimmy James, Stevie-o pulled onto the scene. He stopped near the marina office, climbed out, and stomped toward them.

Kenzie could only assume the sale of the marina wasn't looking good, especially considering the fact that the man who wanted to buy this place just happened to be in town when so much was going wrong.

"I can't believe this," Stevie-o muttered. "I went to take Murphy Bassett to dinner, and no sooner did we leave than I get a call to come back."

"I can only imagine how frustrating this must be," Kenzie murmured.

"I heard someone did this on purpose. Once I figure out who it was . . ." Stevie-o fisted his hands at his sides as his nostrils flared. "Did either of you see anybody here?"

Kenzie shook her head. "I didn't. But we'd really just gotten back here when the fire erupted."

Stevie-o let out a breath and glanced around, his cheeks red with frustration. "The only person I saw wandering around here before I left was that deckhand of yours."

"Eddie?" Jimmy James asked.

"No, the other one. Owen."

Owen? Owen was the quiet, unassuming type. Kenzie had pegged him as an introvert, someone who needed time to recharge alone.

"He was probably just killing time until we go back onto the yacht," Kenzie said.

"Maybe." Stevie-o's scowl deepened. "Or maybe he's up to something. As far as I'm concerned, everyone is a suspect. *Everyone.*"

Kenzie's gut twisted at the thought. Could somebody from the yacht be responsible for her abduction? For the fire? It didn't make sense to her.

Then again, the crimes centered at this marina hadn't begun until *Almost Paradise* cruised into town.

She frowned.

Knowing that, she wouldn't be sleeping very well at night.

JIMMY JAMES RAN a hand over his head and let out a breath. What was going on? Why did danger keep nipping at their heels?

He stood on the dock. His life here had, at one time, had seemed so simple. So routine. So ordinary.

Now every time he thought about this place, he thought of danger. Of trouble.

Of loss.

Because he'd almost lost Kenzie more than once.

"Jimmy James?" Kenzie softly placed her hand on his arm, momentarily pulling him from his frustrated thoughts.

His jaw tightened as he searched for the right words. The last thing he wanted to do was add more stress to Kenzie. But he didn't want to withhold the truth from her either.

Instead, he let out a long breath before saying, "I feel like everything is unstable around us, and I don't know how to make things safe again. I don't know how to keep *you* safe."

"It's not your job to keep me safe."

Jimmy James stared into her wide, imploring eyes. How could Kenzie say that? Couldn't she see just how enamored he was with her?

"You know I care about you." His voice cracked as he looked down at her and said the words.

Kenzie tilted her head, her nurturing spirit showing in the gentleness of her gaze. "I know. But if anything happens to me, it's not your fault."

He broke from the trance-like power Kenzie had over him and stepped back. She just didn't get it. She didn't understand his driving propulsion to keep her safe. It almost felt like a need—right up there along with eating and sleeping.

Instead of trying to explain, he ran a hand over his face and let out a long, drawn-out sigh.

"How about we take a walk?" he finally said. "I could stand to blow off some steam."

"I'm good with that."

Her voice seemed to ease some of the tension in his muscles. But he couldn't let himself off the hook so easily. He'd messed up tonight.

His gaze locked with hers. "I left you alone, and you could have been killed."

Kenzie raised her chin, her eyes unwavering. "You left me to go help somebody. You left me at a place that was supposed to be safe. You did nothing wrong."

"I should have known better. I should have known you're not safe anywhere."

"You didn't let him win. As soon as this guy spotted you, he let go of me."

"If I'd been five seconds later, we might not be having this conversation right now." Jimmy James stepped closer and lowered his head. "I'm not trying to scare you, Kenzie. That's the last thing I want. But you and I both need to understand the reality of the situation right now."

For a split second, he saw fear flash in Kenzie's gaze. Just as quickly as it appeared, the emotion was gone. She swallowed hard before saying, "We leave tomorrow. Maybe once I'm on the boat, it'll be better."

Jimmy James gave her a look, hoping she'd see the truth in his gaze. He didn't want to have to say it out loud, but he would if he needed to.

Realization washed over Kenzie's features, and she sucked in a breath. "There's a chance all this is connected to *Almost Paradise*, isn't there?"

He shrugged. "We don't know that."

"You think it could be, don't you?"

Jimmy James remained silent, knowing he'd finally gotten through to her.

But still, that realization didn't make him feel any better.

He wouldn't feel better until Kenzie was no longer in danger.

## CHAPTER TWENTY-TWO

BEFORE JIMMY JAMES and Kenzie reached the gangplank leading to *Almost Paradise*, someone yelled behind them.

Kenzie turned to see Cassidy hurrying toward them. The police chief paused in front of them, sucked in a deep breath, and rubbed her belly.

"When you're pregnant, nothing is as easy as it used to be." She let out another breath. "Anyway, I wanted to let you know we just got a hit on that license plate."

Kenzie held her breath as she waited for the police chief to continue.

Cassidy looked at the pad in her hand. "It belongs to somebody named Mitch Duchy, spelled D-U-C-H-Y. You ever heard the name?"

Kenzie and Jimmy James both shook their heads.

"Is there anything else you can tell us about him?" Kenzie asked, anxious for more details, more answers.

"He's forty-three years old and from Nebraska. He's married but separated. He had a son named Nick who was twenty-three. But he passed away a few months ago."

"I can't say any of that sounds familiar," Jimmy James said.

Cassidy frowned as she slid her pad back into her pocket. "I just thought it was worth asking."

"This man hasn't reported his motorcycle stolen, has he?" Jimmy James asked.

"Not that I've heard. I'm going to keep digging and see what I can find out."

"Thanks for the update," Jimmy James said.

"Of course. You two be safe."

As soon as she was gone, Jimmy James and Kenzie began walking toward the gangplank. Kenzie couldn't stop repeating the man's name in her head. Was it familiar?

She didn't think so. Still, she wanted to see the man's picture. Wanted to know more about him. Maybe his identity was the key to discovering what was going on here.

As soon as they stepped onboard, Jimmy James turned toward her. "Come to the bridge for a few minutes. If you don't mind . . ."

Kenzie didn't ask any questions as she followed him to the wheelhouse. He closed the door behind them and then picked up his laptop computer. The two of them sat on a bench seat at the back of the space, the computer between them. Jimmy James typed the man's name into the search bar and, a moment later, results filled the screen.

Kenzie stared at Mitch Duchy's face. The man didn't look like a killer. He was thin and gawky with light-brown hair and an angular nose. His smile didn't quite reach his eyes, but more in a haggard manner than a psychopathic one.

"Nothing?" Jimmy James glanced at her, studying her expression.

Kenzie shook her head and frowned. "No, nothing."

"Let's keep looking."

They scrolled through some of the man's social media accounts. Up until around six months ago, pictures were posted of Mitch with his family. But those photos had stopped.

Kenzie wondered what had happened. Something must have changed. There were a few messages of condolences for his loss, and one post on his wall even said, "I'm sorry to hear about you and Ann."

Something bad had definitely happened.

An earlier post caught Kenzie's attention. She placed her hand over Jimmy James'. "Click on that."

He did as she asked.

Kenzie leaned closer as she read the long stretch of text. "It looks like Mitch's son had surgery for a brain tumor . . . and he didn't make it."

Jimmy James glanced at her. "Why does that catch your attention?"

Her gaze caught his. "Because that sounds like the kind of surgery my father would do."

His eyes widened. "You think this is somehow connected with your father?"

"I think we need to do more research."

---

JIMMY JAMES LEANED back in his seat and tried to think this through.

A surgery Dr. Anderson performed didn't go as planned, resulting in his patient's death. That death may have also resulted in the breakup of Mitch's marriage if he was reading between the lines correctly. Now, the patient's father had decided to go after the doctor's daughter in retaliation for his losses.

Was that really what was happening?

The whole thing sounded far-fetched. But maybe this guy wanted Kenzie to suffer like his son had suffered. Jimmy James couldn't imagine the emotions Mitch must have dealt with to lead him to this point. Grief could do horrible things to people.

He reached over and squeezed Kenzie's hand. "Are you okay?"

She nodded, even though the motion seemed stiff. "I guess. I don't really know what to think right now."

"Are you going to call your dad?"

She lowered her head, her gaze skimming her lap as she shrugged. "I should. I just don't look forward to talking to him after our last conversation."

Dr. Anderson had come to Lantern Beach the week before to try to talk Kenzie into coming home. When he'd met Jimmy James, he'd been less than thrilled to learn the two of them were interested in each other. Her dad made some biting comments to Jimmy James that had made Jimmy James question if he truly could have a future with Kenzie.

Jimmy James' biggest regret was that he'd allowed the man to get in his head.

"Your relationship with your dad is important," Jimmy James said, his voice mellow but firm. "I don't want anything to come between you—especially not me."

Kenzie nodded, though her mind looked a million miles away. "You're right. Dads are important. I know yours is important to you. I could tell that by the way you talked about him when we were on the beach."

"I can say the same for you—even if you were talking about him teaching you to stitch up wounds."

She let out a laugh, but the sound quickly faded and an apprehensive look filled her gaze.

Jimmy James leaned closer. "I can stay with you if you want."

She frowned before running a hand through her hair. She pressed her lips together, as if still contemplating what she wanted to do. Finally, she said, "Thank you, but I probably need to do this myself."

"Why don't you stay in here then so you can have some privacy?" He stood. "I'll just be outside if you need me or if you want to talk afterward."

"Thank you, Jimmy James." A grateful smile tugged at her lips.

He glanced out the window to check if anyone was nearby.

When he didn't see anyone, he leaned forward and pressed his lips against Kenzie's. He didn't think he'd ever grow tired of her sweet kisses.

With one last lingering look, he left so Kenzie could talk to her father in private. He prayed their conversation went well . . . and if it provided some answers also, that would be the icing on the cake.

# CHAPTER TWENTY-THREE

KENZIE WIPED a palm on her jean shorts as she stared at her phone. She was surprisingly nervous about making this call to her father.

But she had no other choice right now.

Finally, she swallowed and dialed his number.

He answered on the first ring. "Kenzie? Is that you? Is everything okay?"

"Hi, Dad. It's me." She brought her knees to her chest as she pressed herself into her seat.

"I've been hoping you'd call."

Kenzie waited to see if he would apologize for their last conversation, but he didn't.

Part of her wasn't surprised.

She cleared her throat. "I have a question for you."

Her voice sounded slightly cold.

Then she remembered being on that boat and thinking she was going to die. She thought about the regrets she would have had if she did. Regrets like ending her last conversation with her dad in a negative way.

She swallowed hard again, not sure how she wanted to handle this conversation. Maybe it would be better if she just got right to the point.

"Do you know a man named Mitch Duchy?" she asked.

"Duchy, you say? I can't say that name is familiar off the top of my head."

"He had a son named Nick. I believe you may have performed brain surgery on him. However, I don't think that surgery was successful."

Her dad sucked in a breath. "Oh, yes, I remember now. Why are you asking about him? You know there's doctor-patient confidentiality so . . ."

"I know this is going to sound crazy, but I believe Mitch is here on Lantern Beach and that he's possibly targeting me."

"Why would he do that?"

"I don't know. Maybe as revenge for the failed surgery. Was he upset?"

"Yes, he was upset. But every surgery isn't successful, unfortunately. It doesn't matter who the surgeon is. Patients and their families often don't understand, but my team ran through all the possible outcomes with them, and they signed a release before the surgery."

"Do you remember Mr. Duchy having any violent tendencies?"

"He didn't threaten me or punch me if that's what you're asking." Her dad paused. "You really think he's on the island and trying to hurt you?"

Kenzie nibbled on her lip as she considered how much to say. If she admitted she'd been set adrift in the ocean, her dad might rush back to Lantern Beach and force her to go home with him. Part of her wouldn't even blame him.

"He was in the parking lot here at the marina taking pictures," she finally said. "We got his license plate number and ran it. That's how we came up with his name."

"Taking pictures of you?"

"That's how it appeared."

"I certainly don't like the sound of that," her dad said.

"Neither do I."

Kenzie glanced out the window, wondering what to say next and hating the fact that the conversation sounded so strained. At one time, the two of them had been able to talk easily. But now it felt like an ocean stretched between them.

"I should call the police chief back and tell her about the connection," Kenzie finally said. "I just wanted to talk to you first."

"Kenzie . . ." Her father's voice trailed.

Her throat ached as she swallowed. "Look, I love you, Dad. And I'll always love you. Just know that, okay?"

"But Kenzie—"

She knew by the sound of his voice that he was about to try to convince her to see things his way again. She didn't have the energy to argue with him right now.

"I've gotta run," she blurted. "I'll talk to you later."

Before he could hound her anymore, she hit End.

Conversation done.

Despite the fact the two of them had talked, regret still haunted her.

What if she and her dad never overcame their differences?

A FEW MINUTES LATER, Jimmy James saw Kenzie motion for him to come back to the bridge. Based on her stiff motions, her conversation hadn't gone well. He pressed his lips together, hoping that wasn't the case.

He sat beside Kenzie as she filled him in on her conversation with her father. Her trembling voice made it clear she was having a hard time dealing with this rift between her and her dad.

Jimmy James wished he could somehow fix the situation, but he knew he couldn't. He had to let Kenzie fix this.

When Kenzie finished, the two of them called Chief Chambers. She assured them she'd look into the connection between Mitch and Kenzie's father.

As they wrapped up the conversation, Jimmy James couldn't help but conclude that if Mitch was guilty in this, the boat was the safest place Kenzie could be.

But he had to wonder about Owen being at the marina right before the fire.

A lot of things still didn't fit. Like, would this Mitch guy really go so far as to light that boat on fire, potentially killing someone else, in order to grab Kenzie?

There remained too many questions without answers. But maybe they were inching closer.

Kenzie let out a sigh and stood. "I guess I should turn in for the night. We're going to have a few long days ahead of us."

Jimmy James stood also and closed the space between them. He wanted nothing more than to take her into his arms. But as he saw Eddie walk past the window, he stopped himself.

"I'll see you in the morning," Jimmy James stiffly told Kenzie instead.

She offered a soft, sweet smile. "Have a good night, Captain."

Jimmy James followed her to the doorway, and his gaze trailed her as she disappeared. From the other side of the boat, just out of sight, he heard Eddie talking to someone. He must be on the phone because Jimmy James could only hear part of the conversation.

"I've got this under control," Eddie muttered. "Trust me. I know. Believe me, I know. I'm on top of it."

On top of it? What exactly was his first mate on top of?

Jimmy James stepped closer, trying to hear more of the conversation.

Before he could, someone appeared in the doorway.

Araminta. She smiled brightly as she stepped closer to him. "Hello, Captain Gamble."

His throat tightened. This woman screamed trouble—and trouble was exactly what he wanted to stay away from. He couldn't pinpoint exactly what it was other than pure gut instinct. But she gave off a vixen vibe.

He remained stiff as he said, "Good evening, Araminta."

"I just wanted to let you know I'm really looking forward to working with you on this charter. I know me turning up here is a bit of a surprise. But you won't be disappointed."

The look she gave him made Jimmy James' defenses rise. Her timing couldn't be worse.

He glanced behind him toward Eddie, but his first mate had already walked away.

Whatever he'd been talking about . . . Jimmy James wouldn't be overhearing any more of that conversation.

He frowned as he turned back to Araminta.

Now he needed to figure out how to slip away

without causing a scene. Too much one-on-one attention to the woman wouldn't be helpful.

And the last thing he wanted was for her to get the wrong idea.

# CHAPTER TWENTY-FOUR

PROMPTLY AT NINE a.m. the next morning, the crew lined up on the dock in their whites and greeted their guests, the Abernathy party.

Afterward, the crew helped load the luggage onto the boat while Sunni gave the Abernathys a tour of the yacht and allowed them to choose their rooms. As they began their voyage out to sea, their guests met on the aft deck for snacks and drinks while Araminta and Kenzie unpacked for them.

Kenzie had been assigned to Mr. and Mrs. Abernathy's stateroom.

She carefully unpacked their suitcases—they'd brought five—and placed their clothes in drawers or hung them in the closet. Several items would need to be ironed as well.

She paused when she saw Mrs. Abernathy's jewelry case. She'd been very clear with her instructions that she wanted her pieces stored in the top drawer of the dresser, on the velvety fabric there.

Kenzie's eyes widened when she opened the jewelry box and saw everything inside. The woman had some really beautiful pieces. Icicle diamond earrings. An emerald lavaliere. Uncountable rings, all dotted with precious gemstones.

Kenzie supposed if someone owned a chain of jewelry stores, she should expect them to travel with a lot of bling. Kenzie herself wasn't a big jewelry person, mostly just the diamond earrings she always wore that had once belonged to her mother.

When she finished unpacking, she quickly put the suitcases in a storage area, took one last look at the master stateroom to make sure it was straight, and then went to help with the other rooms.

She tried her best to relax. But she couldn't deny that her lungs still felt tight. The slight sunburn she had on her cheeks and shoulders served as a temporary scar of the attempt on her life. The fear she felt with every footstep was a constant reminder that someone had nearly abducted her again.

Kenzie knew better than to think she could bounce back from that ordeal in one or two days.

She'd learned in med school what trauma did to the brain. But, right now, she hoped staying busy would be her best therapy.

Meanwhile, she hoped Cassidy was having some luck tracking down Mitch. If she could locate him, maybe they'd have answers. Maybe they could finally move forward.

After she finished the other staterooms, she headed to the aft deck to see if Sunni needed help serving. As she did, she quickly glanced at her phone.

Kenzie released her breath when she saw that she hadn't received any more threats.

That was an answer to prayer at least.

But as she passed the main salon, she saw Jimmy James standing outside it. Before he saw her, his phone rang, and he put it to his ear. A moment later his eyes narrowed as if he'd received bad news.

Then he strode away from the salon and toward the bridge.

What was going on? Did this have to do with her abduction?

Whatever it was, she prayed everything was okay.

JIMMY JAMES STEPPED toward the bridge as soon as he saw the name pop up on his phone screen. "Hey, Pops. What's going on?"

He tried to call his dad every week or so, but if his dad called him, it was usually because something was wrong. His dad was a man of few words.

"You'll never believe this," his dad started. "Remember those tests that I had done last year?"

Jimmy James remembered them well. The doctor had thought that his father might have lung cancer. He had gone through a gamut of tests, MRIs, and biopsies to see if the spots were indeed tumors. The good news was that no cancer had been found.

"I remember."

"I've been getting the bills for the testing, but I haven't been able to pay them. It all adds up to almost twenty thousand dollars."

"Twenty thousand dollars? Just for tests? Doesn't your insurance cover that?"

"Apparently, they didn't approve the tests."

"It's a little late for them to tell you this now." Jimmy James stood behind the helm, grateful to have some privacy for this conversation.

"I know. But it doesn't matter now because what's done is done." His dad's voice sounded weaker than it once had. Aging—and being a chronic smoker—hadn't been good to his father.

"How are you going to pay for those tests if insurance won't cover it?"

"That's what I'm trying to figure out. But the medical center has put a lien on my house and is threatening to take away my home if I don't pay up."

"What? They can't do that."

"They say that they can. They say that they *will*."

"Dad . . ." Jimmy James didn't know what else to say. "I don't want that to happen. But if it does, you know you can always come stay with me."

"I'm not going to come stay with you!" His voice rose with every word. "This is my house. I saved my money to buy it. And I'm not going to let anyone take it away from me."

"How do you plan on paying? You sold your boat. Your car is probably only worth a couple thousand dollars at most. Your house is the only thing of value. Did you ask about a payment plan of some sort?"

"They mentioned one to me, but it was still going to be about five hundred dollars a month. If I pay five hundred dollars a month, I won't have money for groceries."

His stomach clenched. That wasn't what he wanted to hear.

Jimmy James thought about the money he'd been saving for his own boat. For a bigger boat. A boat he could do more with.

If he gave his father that money, maybe his dad would be able to keep his house. His father had moved to Georgia three years ago after he met a woman there online. Their relationship hadn't lasted, but his dad had loved the retirement community and decided to stay.

But if Jimmy James gave up all his savings, he'd be back to starting from scratch. Working the docks. Because he knew this job on *Almost Paradise* wouldn't last forever. He had to have a plan for after this contract ended.

He thought he did have a plan. But if his dad needed his help . . .

"We're going to figure out something," Jimmy James said. "Just hold on for a couple of days while I try to figure out what to do."

"Thanks, Son. I knew if anyone could help me, it was you."

Jimmy James put his phone away and stared out to sea.

Giving up his savings to pay for those medical bills was something he'd do if he had to. But the thought of it made him feel defeated. He'd worked so hard to save that money. He knew he could do it again. But he also knew that would mean his own dreams would be delayed.

What would that mean for Kenzie? Would she care if Jimmy James simply remained a dockworker? He wouldn't be able to take her out for fancy dinners or on expensive vacations. Living on a budget could be challenging. And his impression after talking to Kenzie was that she'd never really wanted for anything—not until now that she'd walked away from med school.

More doubts pummeled him. He tried to push them away, but he couldn't.

He had some big decisions he needed to make.

# CHAPTER TWENTY-FIVE

A FEW HOURS LATER, their guests had eaten lunch and *Almost Paradise* had traveled farther down the coast. They were going to drop anchor for the evening so the Abernathys could take the water toys out.

Kenzie supposed that the Abernathys seemed nice enough, although in a very shallow way.

There was a huge difference between people who were filthy rich and people who were simply well-off. Most people would consider her father, a successful surgeon, to be wealthy. But, even as a surgeon, her father didn't drop a hundred thousand dollars to charter a yacht for a few days. This was an entirely different kind of mindset.

As Kenzie grabbed some water bottles to take to

the swim deck, her mind went to the conversation she'd seen Jimmy James having on the phone. She'd passed him a couple of times since then, and he hadn't said anything to her about it.

That led Kenzie to believe it wasn't Cassidy calling with an update. Maybe it had been something of a more personal nature. In truth, his conversations weren't any of her business. But she did hope Jimmy James might share what it was about, especially since he'd looked upset.

She pushed those thoughts aside as she set the water bottles on the swim deck and glanced out at everyone having fun on the Jet Skis and clear-bottom kayaks. Even though the main goal of the family was to head to Florida, they did want to have some fun on the way. This was part of their itinerary.

With all her immediate tasks finished, Kenzie leaned on the rail and watched them. As she did, footsteps sounded behind her, and she nearly jumped out of her skin.

"I didn't mean to scare you," a deep voice said.

She looked behind her and saw Roman Abernathy standing there in his swimsuit, shaking water off his hair with a towel. The man was blond with sculpted abs, a wide smile, and evenly spaced features.

Kenzie was sure women went wild for him. He had a certain air about him—a confidence—that a lot of women were no doubt drawn to.

"Oh, don't apologize," Kenzie said. "It's me. I have a tendency to be a little jumpy."

He joined her at the railing and watched his father and the rest of the group play in the water. "They're just like overgrown teenagers sometimes."

"Not you?"

"Not when I'm around them." Roman flashed a grin.

"It's nice that you're here joining them on the charter."

He shrugged as if it weren't a big deal. "My family isn't traditional. Since my old man is training me to take over the business one day, I figured I should probably see what it's all about."

"That's not what you want to do?" Kenzie's throat burned as she asked the question. She understood what it was like to be shoved down a path you didn't want to travel.

"I don't really know yet." Roman's thick brows jutted together in thought. "Part of me thinks it would be pretty cool. Another part of me just likes having fun. There will be enough time to get serious and settle down later, right?"

"That's one way of looking at things." On one hand, she could see his viewpoint. On the other, Kenzie had never wanted anything for free. Most people thought she was just a spoiled rich girl, but her father had made her pay her own way to med school. Primarily, she'd done so through academic scholarships. But having a good work ethic was something her mom had instilled in her.

Kenzie felt Roman's gaze on her.

"You don't agree?" He leaned against the rail, watching her as if he really wanted to hear her viewpoint.

She shrugged. "I think we all take different paths. The important thing is at the end of the day you can live with yourself and your choices."

He nodded slowly. "It almost sounds like you understand."

She nibbled on her lip a moment, wondering how much she should share. She didn't usually open up to guests. But Roman was the one who'd initiated this conversation.

Finally, she said, "I decided not to go back to med school and follow in my father's footsteps."

He let out a low whistle. "You do understand then."

"I guess I do."

He nodded toward the interior of the boat. "You just want to work on a yacht instead?"

She glanced around at *Almost Paradise*. "I can't say I'll do this for the rest of my life. It would be really hard to ever have a family one day and work on one of these. But I know I don't want to go into medicine. I'm not passionate about it. In fact, medical procedures make me pretty anxious sometimes. I just don't think it's the career for me."

"It's good that you realize that. I know that there can be a lot of pressure in things like this. I actually thought about going to med school at one time."

"But you changed your mind, I guess?"

"I did. I know I'm supposed to have things figured out by now, but I guess I don't."

Kenzie smiled at him. In some ways, she felt like she could relate to this guy.

Just then, the rest of Roman's family headed back toward the boat. It was time for them to get cleaned up for dinner.

Roman seemed to realize that and straightened. "It was good talking to you, Kenzie."

"Yes, it was good talking to you too. I'll see you again later."

JIMMY JAMES COULDN'T STOP THINKING about seeing Kenzie and Roman together.

He'd come to find her to tell her about the phone call with his dad. Instead, he'd stopped before anyone had seen him. He watched as Kenzie and Roman leaned on the railing and talked as if they were good friends.

He tried not to think too much of it.

But a nagging voice inside his head kept telling him that Roman was the kind of person Kenzie needed to be with.

He hated when his insecurity reared its head. There weren't many things that could set it off, but issues of class and money usually could.

He'd told Kenzie from the start that she needed someone who could provide the kind of life she was accustomed to. That he wouldn't be able to give her the finer things in life.

But someone like Roman could. The two of them were cut from the same cloth, after all.

What if Jimmy James was just some type of fling for Kenzie? What if she was just being rebellious and part of that rebellion included dating the bad boy?

He thought he knew Kenzie well enough to say

she wouldn't do that. But he couldn't be a hundred percent sure.

He slipped away before either Kenzie or Roman saw him.

As soon as all the water toys were back in the boat, Jimmy James would continue on down the coast. Tomorrow they'd stop in Charleston quickly before departing again the next day.

This should be a simple trip. At least, he prayed that was the case.

But as he headed to the bridge to get ready to go, a commotion in the salon caught his ear. What was going on now?

He stepped inside and saw Mrs. Abernathy standing in the center of the room, a bathrobe wrapped around her body and her eyes lit with accusation as she stared at Sunni and Araminta. Other guests and crew members flooded into the room to see what the fuss was about.

"What's going on here?" Jimmy James asked.

Mrs. Abernathy glanced at him, outrage saturating her gaze. "One of my necklaces is missing. I demand you find out who took it."

# CHAPTER TWENTY-SIX

KENZIE HEARD RISING voices in the salon and braced herself for whatever might be going on.

She paced from the deck into the room in time to see Mrs. Abernathy waving her hands in the air as she touched her neck. "My favorite necklace is gone. It was in my dresser earlier. I saw it."

Jimmy James turned to everyone in the salon—which appeared to be nearly everyone on the boat. "Has anyone else seen her necklace?"

They all shook their heads no.

"Has anyone been in her room to do a turn-down?" Jimmy James continued.

"Not yet," Sunni answered.

Jimmy James' eyes narrowed with thought as he

turned back to Mrs. Abernathy. "Are you sure you saw it in the dresser?"

"I'm sure. It was there earlier. I'm certain of it."

"Very well." Jimmy James looked at each of his crew members. "I want everyone to split up, and we're going to search every inch of this boat until we find that necklace, crew quarters included. Does everyone understand?"

"Yes, Captain" went around the group.

He turned back to Mrs. Abernathy. "If that necklace is on the boat, we'll find it."

"You better. Or else I *will* be calling and reporting this boat to the proper authorities." Her eyes flashed with more anger.

Tension stretched across Kenzie's chest. This woman was mad, and rightfully so if a piece of valuable jewelry had disappeared.

But who on this boat would have taken it? Could one of the crew members really be responsible?

Kenzie wasn't sure exactly what was going on here.

But Jimmy James split the group up to search.

She hoped this was nothing. But on *Almost Paradise*, that was hardly ever the case.

JIMMY JAMES COULDN'T BELIEVE a necklace disappeared. Who would have taken it?

He didn't want to think anyone on the crew might be responsible.

But he had no doubt that Mrs. Abernathy's threat was true. If they didn't find her necklace, she would report them.

He was going to go through the crew's rooms himself just to make sure that none of his people had anything to do with this.

He started with Owen and Eddie's bunkroom. He opened the first drawer and riffled through the clothing there.

When he got to the last drawer, he paused. A pair of white gloves had been stuffed out of sight in the corner.

White gloves? Why would Eddie or Owen bring white gloves onboard? They almost reminded him of the kind used in a magic show or something.

The accessory might not be suspicious, but they did make him curious.

Kenzie and Sunni's room was next. But before he reached their door, Owen rushed down the stairs and toward him. His curly brown hair bounced as he paused in front of Jimmy James.

"She found it," Owen announced, sucking in a deep breath.

"The necklace? Who found it?"

"Mrs. Abernathy."

Jimmy James straightened his back as he waited to hear more. "Where was it?"

"You'll never believe this, but it was in her dresser the whole time."

A knot formed between Jimmy James' eyes. Had Mrs. Abernathy had so much to drink that she hadn't noticed the necklace was right where she'd left it?

He didn't know what was going on here.

But he'd give anything to have one charter that wasn't filled with drama.

# CHAPTER TWENTY-SEVEN

THAT NIGHT after all their guests had been served, several crew members gathered in the crew mess to unwind before going to bed. Owen was the only one not there, and that was because he had anchor watch, which meant he'd guard the boat to make sure trouble didn't arise while everyone was sleeping.

The rest of them would be up early to begin their daily tasks. Working on a luxury yacht was definitely a thankless job, one in which the crew got little sleep, breaks, or acknowledgment.

Kenzie had joined the rest of the group, who all feasted on some chicken fettuccini Chef Durango had made. There were also breadsticks, tossed salads, and brownies. Everything tasted—and smelled—delicious. There were perks to working with a five-star chef—even if the man did insist on talking with a fake French accent, hoping it would make people take him more seriously. He still used it in front of the crew, but he really turned it on in front of guests.

Sometimes, she couldn't help but reflect on how working on this boat was similar to the premise of one of her favorite shows—*Downton Abbey*. On the upper decks, the rich flaunted their wealth while being waited on hand and foot. Belowdecks was where the hospitality workers—who in some ways were similar to servants—lived and encountered their own drama.

The differences in classes could definitely be felt, even in a day and age when classes weren't supposed to be as prominent.

"Can you believe that necklace was there the whole time?" Eddie asked before taking a bite of his pasta.

"Maybe Roselyn is just all drama." Sunni waved a breadstick in the air. "Maybe she's the kind of person who thinks nothing is ever her fault. Did you see the accusation in her eyes?"

"She was serious when she threatened to report

us." Araminta raised her eyebrows as she gave everyone a pointed look.

Kenzie tried not to be too judgmental of people, but Araminta drove her crazy. She liked working on this boat a lot more when it was just her and Sunni as stews. Araminta added a little too much drama to the mix.

"You're being quiet over there, Kenzie." Eddie glanced at her. "What do you think about all this? You unpacked Mrs. Abernathy's bags. If anyone was going to be blamed, it would have probably been you."

Kenzie's gut tensed at the words. She knew they were true. Had someone known that and tried to set her up? She couldn't rule that out. Someone who hated her enough to try to kill her wouldn't hesitate to try to frame her for a crime.

Instead of dwelling on it, she pushed her half-eaten dinner away and shrugged. "If I were Mrs. Abernathy, I would have wanted my jewelry put in the safe. I wouldn't have wanted it left unattended in the room. But she specifically asked me to put it in the dresser. I'm still unsure how she missed that the necklace was right where it was supposed to be."

The whole thing didn't make sense to Kenzie—

unless Mrs. Abernathy was just trying to start trouble. But why would she do that? For attention?

"Maybe I need to get out of this line of work," Sunni said. "There's too much crazy in this profession."

"Speaking of which . . . what are you all going to do after this charter season ends?" Araminta stole a cherry tomato from Sunni's salad and took a bite. "I know we're only halfway through. But have you guys made any plans for after this is done?"

"I want to go to Bali," Sunni said. "Maybe I'll just get a job waitressing there until I figure things out."

"I thought about working on the fishing boats in Alaska," Eddie said. "I heard you can make some pretty good money up there in the off-season."

"What about you, Kenzie?" Araminta turned toward her.

Kenzie felt herself bristle. Araminta had made no effort to be her friend so the fact she was asking sent up red flags. She felt certain the woman had some sort of ulterior motive.

However, Kenzie had no idea how to answer her question about the future. She'd set the first part of her plan in motion. That included leaving med school to take this job. But what happened after this season ended wasn't at the forefront of her mind.

She was usually a planner. She liked to know where the road would take her. But in this case, the answers hadn't come to her yet. Hopefully they would soon.

"I'm still trying to figure that out." Kenzie reached forward and twirled a piece of pasta around her fork, desperate for a distraction from this conversation.

"You can stay in Lantern Beach with Captain Gamble." Sunni waggled her eyebrows.

Clearly, the crew all knew there was something between them. But Kenzie wasn't going to admit it.

"I do like Lantern Beach," Kenzie said.

"And Captain Gamble," Sunni added.

Araminta visibly bristled beside her as if she didn't like hearing that.

Kenzie needed to change the subject before the woman started a cat fight.

She seemed the type.

Kenzie cleared her throat. "By the way, have any of you guys ever met Mr. Robertson?"

"Not face-to-face." Eddie dished up a second helping, his stomach seeming like a bottomless pit. "Why?"

"I'm just wondering what this guy is like." Kenzie

tried to sound casual. "One of you guys mentioned he was kind of eccentric."

"Anyone who wants to bring a superyacht to Lantern Beach has to be a little bit eccentric." Sunni snorted.

"I can see that. It's definitely not your typical yacht destination." Usually, guests on yachts liked to go to high-end places, locations much fancier than Lantern Beach.

"A lot of times the captain and crew never meet the luxury yacht owner," Eddie said between bites. "The owner usually uses a management firm to oversee the staff. Mr. Robertson, however, likes to be hands-on."

"Do you think *Almost Paradise* will stay at Lantern Beach?" Kenzie didn't know how much the rest of the crew knew about Bassett's plan for the marina. She and Jimmy James had told Eddie, and she assumed he could have mentioned it to the others. She, however, was not going to bring it up.

"That's a good question. But I really have no idea." Eddie rose and lifted his plate, carrying it toward the sink. "I think it's time for me to turn in for the night. I'll see everyone in the morning."

Kenzie hadn't learned anything new from listening to the rest of the crew.

But their conversation had been a good reminder that she needed to start thinking about what her future was going to look like after this job was done.

---

THE NEXT MORNING, just as the sun started to spill over the horizon, Jimmy James drank a cup of black coffee and sat on the bridge of *Almost Paradise* as they continued south. In only an hour or so they would reach Charleston.

He'd gotten little sleep last night as his mind raced through everything that had happened over the past few days: Kenzie being abducted and set adrift, the man taking photos of her, the marina fire, the second abduction attempt.

Last night, he'd checked the security camera footage to see who'd gone into Mrs. Abernathy's room around the time her necklace had disappeared. However, there had been a glitch during a thirty-minute period.

The footage offered him no information. Even worse—had someone tampered with the equipment in order to avoid being caught? Or had nothing happened? Had Mrs. Abernathy simply been mistaken?

He sighed. Each event almost seemed surreal.

Plus, Jimmy James had talked to Chief Chambers last night. Sometime today, he would find a free moment with Kenzie and give her an update on that conversation.

Almost as if she'd read his mind, a knock sounded on the door behind him. His heart quickened when he saw Kenzie standing there wearing a blue *Almost Paradise* polo and black shorts. Her hair still held a touch of dampness, and, even from a distance, he could smell the clean scent of her flowery soap.

"May I come in?" she asked.

He cleared his throat, trying to get his thoughts back into focus. "Of course."

She stepped onto the bridge, two cups of coffee in hand. She nodded to his hand. "I see you already have some."

"As someone wise once told me, you can never have too much coffee." He took one of the cups before shutting the door behind her.

"I hope you don't mind me showing up. But Sunni was still sleeping, and I figured you'd be up already." She held her own cup to her lips but didn't take a sip. Instead, she nodded out the window. "The sunrise is just gorgeous this morning, isn't it?"

"Yes, it is." Jimmy James didn't bother to mention that the sunrise didn't begin to compare to her. He feared those words would sound too much like a line or insincere. But they weren't.

Jimmy James wished the two of them could simply use this moment to flirt. To maybe steal a kiss.

But too many other things were going on—more serious things.

"I'm glad you're here," Jimmy James started. "There are some things I wanted to talk to you about."

"Is it about the phone call you got yesterday?" Kenzie sat down on the bench seat.

It took Jimmy James a moment to remember what she was talking about. But then his conversation with his dad flooded back into his mind. Kenzie had been close when he'd gotten the call.

Jimmy James sat at the helm, turning in his chair to face her. "Ahh, that. That was my dad."

"Is everything okay?" Kenzie stared at him, a crease of concern forming between her eyes.

Jimmy James took another sip of his coffee as he considered what to say. "Truthfully, he's gotten himself up to his eyeballs in some medical bills, and we're trying to figure out what to do about that."

"Medical bills? I didn't realize he'd been sick. There are organizations that might be able to help."

"The tests showed it wasn't cancer, so that's the good news. But all the procedures . . . they cost a lot. I've been saving some money, and if I have to use that, I will."

"You mean, the money you've been saving for your boat?" Surprise raced through Kenzie's voice.

His jaw twitched as she vocalized what was on the line. Hearing it out loud made him feel the sting of regret. But he had to do what he had to do. "Yes, the money for my boat. If it means my dad has a better quality of life because he gets to keep his house, then that's more important than me buying a boat."

More surprise flashed through her gaze.

Would Kenzie see him in a different light if he gave away the paltry amount of money he'd saved?

He didn't want to believe it, but it was a possibility.

He remembered seeing her and Roman talking yesterday. He wished he could say seeing them interact didn't bother him. But he'd be lying to himself if he did.

Roman could give Kenzie the kind of life she deserved. He didn't want to go down this rabbit hole again. But he'd be a fool not to acknowledge the truth in the situation.

Jimmy James was working so hard to do better, to be better . . . but what if he never moved beyond being a dockworker? The position had no prestige. Little money. And it promised his budget would always be tight, with little room for extras and no room for luxuries.

Jimmy James cleared his throat and shifted, wishing that wasn't the truth. But this wasn't the time he wanted to talk about it. "Actually, I wanted to chat with you about a phone call I got late last night from Chief Chambers."

Kenzie's eyes widened at the mention of the police chief. "Cassidy? What did she say?"

"She was able to track down Mitch Duchy."

"Wait . . . she actually found him? Questioned him?" Hope lilted in her voice.

Jimmy James nodded, wanting to quickly douse her hope before she read too much into his statement. "She did. But it's not all good news."

Kenzie leaned back and waited for him to continue. "What do you mean?"

"Mitch—Mr. Duchy—admitted that he did come to Lantern Beach and he took some pictures of you.

He was going to send those pictures to your father but only as an empty threat."

"Isn't that what every criminal says?"

"You can't count on criminals to tell the truth, that's for sure. But this guy has a strong alibi for the day you were abducted and set adrift."

She shoved her eyebrows together. "Like what?"

"He was in court for a traffic violation."

"Really?" Disbelief stretched through her voice. "So, he isn't the one who abducted me? What about the fire on the boat?"

Jimmy James somberly shook his head. "It doesn't look like it."

Kenzie's hand went over her mouth, and her eyes remained wide. "But . . . if Mitch wasn't behind it, then who was?"

# CHAPTER TWENTY-EIGHT

KENZIE STOOD as Jimmy James got a call on his radio. He clearly needed to get back to work.

She waved a quick goodbye to him, pausing only for a moment as he waved back.

She wasn't sure what she was hoping for. Maybe a quick kiss. A moment of connection.

But their talk had been interrupted.

She continued from the bridge, heading toward the galley to begin her shift. As she walked, she reflected on their conversation.

Kenzie thought it was really sweet he wanted to use his savings to pay his father's medical bills. But she also knew Jimmy James had worked so hard to save that money, to try to achieve his dreams. It seemed a shame all that would change so quickly.

There had to be another way for his father to pay the bills, for his father to get the money he needed.

Kenzie's mind continued to race as she tried to think of some solutions.

She also had to admit that she was bothered by the whole Mitch situation. It had seemed like a slam dunk that he was the one behind what happened.

But if not Mitch, then who? Kenzie didn't even have any really good guesses. The only other person whose name came to mind was Owen, but she had a hard time believing he'd do something like this. He seemed too reserved, too nice. But he had been spotted at the marina right before the fire.

If she ruled out Owen and Mitch, who were the other possibilities?

Eddie? Araminta?

She just couldn't say for sure. She didn't want to believe anyone could be involved. But being a Pollyanna would only get her killed right now.

She'd need to keep her eyes wide open.

As Kenzie stepped into the galley to help start serving food for breakfast, she put the thoughts aside.

But her questions would never be far from her mind . . . because her life depended on finding those answers.

A LITTLE OVER AN HOUR LATER, *Almost Paradise* docked in Charleston.

As Jimmy James readied himself to disembark, he mentally reviewed the upcoming schedule. The Abernathys wanted to explore the area for a few hours, including having lunch at a popular seafood restaurant.

Part of the crew would stay on the boat to clean while others would join the family on their excursion.

Kenzie had requested to be one of the crew members going into town. Jimmy James had some reservations about that, considering everything going on. But he didn't want to be overbearing either.

That meant he would be exploring Charleston with the Abernathys as well—just so he could keep an eye on Kenzie.

Jimmy James smoothed his bright-blue polo shirt and stepped onto the deck, heading toward the gangplank so he could join the Abernathys. As soon as he left the bridge, someone called to him.

"Hi, Captain Gamble."

He looked up and saw Araminta standing on the deck, almost as if she'd been waiting for him.

He forced a smile. "Hi, Araminta."

She stepped closer, her calculating eyes setting him on edge. "You're looking quite dapper today."

He smoothed his shirt again, trying to politely get out of this conversation. "Thank you."

"I want to be a captain one day, you know. I'd love if you could give me some tips sometime. I could really learn a lot from someone as experienced as you are." Her voice held subtle undertones that she was interested in him in more than a professional way.

His throat tightened. "Maybe when our charter is over."

That seemed like a safe enough answer. But when Araminta's eyes lit, Jimmy James feared she'd taken his words the wrong way.

"I'd like that." She lowered her eyelids, almost in a seductive manner.

"We can talk in a purely professional manner," he added, needing to dispel any misconceptions. He'd dealt with women like her before and knew that clear boundaries were key.

Some of the excitement left Araminta's eyes. But just as quickly as the light faded, a new hope appeared. She leaned closer and whispered, "When I see something I want, I go for it."

Was she talking about getting her captain's license?

Or Jimmy James?

He wasn't sure.

Thankfully, Eddie motioned him toward the gangplank.

Jimmy James was ready to get rid of this woman . . . because he knew her type.

She would do anything to get what she wanted.

That thought didn't comfort him. Not one bit.

As he glanced behind him, he saw Kenzie disappear inside with a tray of drinks.

How long had she been behind him? Had she seen or overheard his conversation with Araminta?

He wasn't sure. But dread filled his stomach at the thought.

# CHAPTER TWENTY-NINE

WHILE THE ABERNATHYS were occupied at the restaurant, Kenzie slipped outside. The crew didn't need to be present during lunch, especially since they weren't joining them. The restaurant was too crowded to have extra people milling around, so Jimmy James had given everyone an hour of free time.

She needed to quickly visit a store on the next street. As she hurried there, she couldn't stop thinking about the interaction she'd seen before disembarking *Almost Paradise*.

Araminta had clearly been flirting with Jimmy James. The woman had made no secret about her interest in him. She sent him flirty smiles. Gave him lingering glances. Talked to him whenever she had the chance.

Nothing about her actions were shy. Araminta wanted Jimmy James to know she was interested.

Jimmy James had remained professional. But still it bothered Kenzie, whether she wanted it to or not.

Araminta didn't seem like the type to give up easily. Kenzie had to wonder at times if Araminta was more of Jimmy James' type—a little wilder, less reserved. The woman probably had a past of her own, a past she was proud of.

Kenzie's past? She'd mostly been a goody-two-shoes.

Kenzie couldn't let Araminta bother her. Right now, she had other things to worry about.

She paused outside of a place called Charlie Town's Pawn and glanced at the flashing red sign atop the building. As she slipped inside, she pushed down a flutter of nerves.

She'd never been to a pawnshop before. She'd never had a reason.

But this place looked nicer than she expected. Everything was organized in neat rows, the walls were a clean white, and the floor was polished cement.

The employee behind the counter appeared to be in his forties, with light brown hair and a clean-shaven face. He almost looked snooty as he appraised her.

He offered a terse smile as he observed her. "Can I help you?"

"I'm hoping you can." She paused by the glass display that also served as the checkout area. "I was wondering how much I could get for these."

She took the diamond earrings from her ears and placed them on the counter.

The man picked one up and held it to the light, letting out a grunt. "These look old. Are you sure you want to get rid of them?"

Kenzie wasn't sure at all. She wanted to at least explore the possibility.

If what her dad told her was correct, these earrings were valuable. They could help ease some of the financial burden that Jimmy James and his dad were experiencing. Then Jimmy James could keep the money he'd saved to buy the boat of his dreams.

These earrings were important to Kenzie, but not because of their financial value. Their sentimental value made her never want to give them up. But she tried not to hold on too tightly to the things of this world. All that stuff was—temporary. The memories she held in her heart of her mother were more important.

Plus, if Kenzie understood correctly, she could buy back these earrings before a certain amount of time passed. She just had to pay the money she'd been given, plus some interest.

She wasn't sure what she wanted to do, and she wrestled with the thought. But at least the possibility should be explored.

The man pulled out a jeweler's loupe and put it to his eye. He then turned on a high-powered lamp and set the earrings under its light as he examined them.

He didn't say anything for several minutes, only letting out the occasional grunt.

Kenzie waited, trying to be patient. Finally, he clicked the light off and looked at her, pushing the earrings back across the glass counter toward her.

"I could give you thirty bucks for these."

Her mouth dropped open. "Thirty bucks? What are you talking about?"

"Those are moissanite."

"Moissanite?" She wasn't sure she'd ever even heard that word.

"Yeah, you know—silicon carbide. It's like cubic zirconia, only better. Anyway, the craftsmanship on these earrings is good, and most people will think they're diamonds. But any experienced jeweler will tell you these stones aren't real. The gold appears to be real, but there's not much of it. I'm sorry, but that's my best price."

"These were my mom's." Kenzie shook her head, refusing to believe the man's words. He was wrong. "My dad gave them to her. They're real."

"Listen, kid, I'm sorry. But those diamonds are as real as Bigfoot. And if you find someone who tells you otherwise, they're lying to you."

---

JIMMY JAMES WATCHED as Kenzie came back around the corner. He didn't want to follow her. Didn't want to be a creep. But how could he not worry about her after everything that had happened?

He'd seen her go into the pawnshop. Why would she go into that store? It didn't make sense. Did Kenzie even have anything to pawn?

Jimmy James knew her well enough to be certain

she wasn't the kind of person to steal something and try to get money from it.

But the only thing she had worth any value seemed to be her mom's earrings.

As Kenzie headed toward him, she glanced up and spotted him. Surprise flooded her gaze before she slowed her steps and frowned. Finally, she continued his way.

After reaching him, she paused in front of him and pressed her lips together as if unsure what to say. Finally, she shook her head, her gaze appearing burdened and full of secrets.

Kenzie had always seemed like an open book, not like the type to hide things. He didn't like the feeling in his gut.

"I was hoping you wouldn't see where I went," she finally said.

"What's going on, Kenzie?" he asked cautiously.

"It's . . . a long story."

"You care to give me the CliffsNotes version?" He knew it might not be his business. But they'd gone through enough together that he didn't feel guilty asking.

Kenzie let out a long breath and looked into the distance as the scent of fudge swirled with the temperate breeze. "I . . . I wanted to see how much my mom's earrings were worth, so I took them into a pawnshop."

Questions flooded his mind, but he didn't ask them. Not yet. Instead, he waited for her to continue.

Her expression remained stiff with tension. "The guy behind the counter told me they're not real, that my earrings are fake."

Jimmy James shoved his eyebrows together in confusion. "What?"

"That's what I said too. It doesn't make sense. My mom gave these to me. My dad would have never bought her fake diamonds for a gift. He's not that type of guy."

"Could that guy at the pawnshop have been wrong?"

Kenzie shook her head. "I don't think he was. He seemed pretty confident, and he had some higher-end stuff inside."

Jimmy James' thoughts continued to race. "Did you keep the earrings in sight the whole time? I've heard of the scam where—"

"I never took my eyes off them, if that's what you were going to say. The man at the pawnshop didn't switch the real earrings for fake ones. Besides, it would be hard to switch these earrings out for another pair. I practically have every detail of them memorized." Kenzie reached for one of her earrings and twirled it.

Jimmy James stared at her another moment, wishing he could fix the situation. That he could think of a way to take away her confusion.

But there was nothing.

He finally settled on, "I don't know what to say, Kenzie. To be honest, I'm surprised you'd even want to pawn them."

That's what really didn't make sense to him. Kenzie loved those earrings, mostly for their sentimental value. Was she in some kind of trouble? That was the only reason he could think of that she'd do something like this.

Kenzie's cheeks flushed as she shoved a lock of hair behind her ear. "I wanted to see how much they were worth, just in case I ever needed to know."

He narrowed his eyes as he tried to read between the lines. "You mean, in case you ever needed money?"

Her gaze remained shaded, as if she didn't want him to know all the details. "Something like that. But now I know."

A footstep sounded behind them, and they both turned. Sunni stepped from around the corner.

How long had she been standing there? Had she heard anything they'd said to each other?

Jimmy James hoped not.

"Fancy seeing you two here." Sunni flashed a grin that looked a little too wide. "I was just looking for a T-shirt for my sister. She's always wanted to go to Charleston."

They both stared at her a moment until she nodded to a store in the distance. "I think I'll try that shop over there."

As Sunni disappeared into another store, Jimmy James and Kenzie fell into step beside each other as they walked toward the restaurant. His thoughts continued to race, but he didn't want to push too hard.

Kenzie would open up when she was ready. But the only conclusion he could muster was that Kenzie was stressed about what she'd do when the charter was over—that she was worried about her finances.

"I'm sorry, Kenzie," Jimmy James told her quietly. "If there's anything I can do . . ."

She nodded, but her gaze looked far-off, as if she was trying to process what she'd learned.

Was it a coincidence that a family full of jewelers

just happened to be on the boat at the same time Kenzie made this discovery?

Jimmy James didn't know, but it seemed like something he should keep in mind. Although, if there was something shady going on involving the Abernathys, he couldn't imagine what it might be.

# CHAPTER THIRTY

KENZIE COULDN'T BELIEVE she'd run into Jimmy James while leaving the pawnshop. Knowing him, he'd been keeping an eye on her. He liked to do that. Part of her loved that protective side of him—unless her privacy was on the line, at least.

She'd wanted to keep her visit secret.

Despite that, Kenzie tried to put everything out of her mind so she could concentrate on her job while on the boat. *Almost Paradise* was about to leave the port and continue heading south. She lingered in the main salon, trying to make sure the Abernathys were happy and that their drinks were constantly refilled.

The deckhands were the busiest during departure. The stewards usually just worked the interior

—helping serve drinks and food, keeping things clean, and getting the laundry done. Both jobs were demanding in different ways.

"Hey, Kenzie." Sunni stopped beside her. "I left a cooler from the trip down on the swim platform. Can you go grab it for me?"

"Sure thing." Kenzie put down the tray she held in her hand, one that was now empty after she'd served the drinks.

She started down the stairway, trying to stay out of the deckhands' way as they untied ropes and went through their normal procedures.

As she glanced at the back of the boat, she spotted the cooler.

Kenzie could quickly slip out there without getting in anyone's way, grab the cooler, and get back upstairs.

As she darted forward to grab it, Owen yelled her name.

She glanced up and saw the concern on his face.

The next instant, she felt something surround her ankle as the boat moved forward.

One of the towlines.

Before Kenzie could step back, the rope pulled tight and jerked her from the deck.

Kenzie hit the water and the towline propelled her away from the boat.

She tried to scream for help.

But, before she could, water consumed her as her body plunged into the depths.

---

"MAN OVERBOARD! MAN OVERBOARD!"

As soon as Jimmy James heard the words come through his radio, his spine stiffened.

No captain wanted to hear that on his watch.

He shifted gears, impatient as he waited for the boat to come to a halt. Then he let First Mate Eddie take over and he rushed outside.

"What's going on?" he asked into the radio.

"Kenzie was caught in the towline," Owen said.

Kenzie? In the towline?

Jimmy James' heart pounded harder.

He rushed toward the stern, knowing that every second counted.

When he reached the swim deck, he saw Owen and Araminta frantically trying to get the rope untied.

If that line jerked too hard, it could take off someone's foot.

He glanced into the water, searching for Kenzie.

Finally, he saw her head bob above the water, only to disappear again.

Wasting no time, he threw his radio on the deck and dove into the water. He swam in wide strokes to reach her. To try to untangle her leg before any more damage could be done.

Only when his lungs screamed for air did he surface. As he did, he saw Kenzie bob above the water again.

Not much farther until he reached her.

He dove under the water to increase his speed.

When he surfaced again, Kenzie was right in front of him. He dove under once more and felt around for her foot. He found it and unwrapped the rope from around her ankle, even as she kicked frantically.

Finally, her leg was free.

*Praise God . . .*

He pushed to the surface and grabbed Kenzie, pulling her to his chest to keep her afloat.

She gasped for air, the sound suspending in the air for a moment.

Finally, she let out a cry.

Quickly, his thoughts cleared, and questions rose in his mind.

What had happened to put Kenzie in this position? Why had she even been on the deck while they were departing?

Jimmy James would find out later.

Right now, he just needed to get her back onboard and make sure she was okay.

## CHAPTER THIRTY-ONE

THE PAIN in Kenzie's leg made it hard to think straight.

For the second time in a week, she'd been certain she was going to die.

Everything had happened so fast.

She must have stepped into the rope coil. Then, as *Almost Paradise* moved out, the rope had tightened as the tender boat behind them had been towed. In an instant, Kenzie had been yanked into the water.

Panicking.

Certain she wasn't going to make it.

Barely able to catch her breath.

Feeling like everything was out of her control.

Until the rope had blissfully loosened as if it had

been untied. Then she'd seen Jimmy James dive into the water to untangle her.

Right now, her head rested on his chest as he did the backstroke and tried to get her back to *Almost Paradise*. The water lapped around them, seeming much more peaceful than it had earlier. Shouts filled the air, probably from the deck of the boat.

Had that really happened? The throbbing ache in her ankle made it clear that it had.

Finally, they reached the boat and the crew grabbed them, tugging them onto the deck. As Kenzie sprawled there, she turned and coughed up the remaining water from her lungs. Her body ached at the movement.

That had been close. So, so close.

Jimmy James appeared beside her, his face and clothes dripping wet as he stared down at her.

His eyes traveled down the length of her before stopping at her ankle. She didn't even want to see what it looked like. All she knew was that it hurt like crazy.

"We need to get a medic on this boat." Jimmy James looked up and said, "Now."

"Yes, sir." Owen stood. "I'll call for one."

As he sprinted to make that call, other crew

members gathered around to see what had happened.

"Can you move your foot?" Jimmy James asked Kenzie.

Kenzie held her breath as she attempted to do so, afraid she wouldn't be able to. Then she felt her toes wiggle.

Relief softened her shoulders.

"I don't think your ankle is broken," Jimmy James said. "Maybe just sprained and bruised. But that rope could have taken your whole foot off."

"I know," Kenzie whispered as another ache rushed through her leg.

"Sunni, go get some ice," Jimmy James directed. "I'm going to get Kenzie out of the sun."

As Sunni scrambled away, Jimmy James lifted Kenzie in his arms and carried her to a lounge chair in the shade. He set her on the cushions before lowering himself into the seat beside her.

His gaze locked with hers. "What were you thinking being down here?"

"Sunni sent me to get a cooler. I was just going to grab it and—"

"No one needs to be on the deck except for the deckhands when we're departing."

Kenzie pressed her lips together. "I know. You don't have to lecture me."

"I'm going to lecture you. People have died from stunts like that."

"It wasn't a stunt . . ." Tears rushed into her eyes. She waited for him to continue, but instead Jimmy James pulled her into his arms.

Kenzie buried her face in his chest, wondering how many times her life was going to flash before her eyes before she got the hint that she was knocking at death's door.

---

THE MEDIC CONFIRMED JIMMY JAMES' suspicions. Kenzie had sprained her ankle. She'd need to keep the injury wrapped, iced, and stay off it for a couple of days. But she would be okay.

Thank goodness.

Before they continued with their journey, Jimmy James had a crew meeting on the bridge to talk about the direness of the situation they'd just gone through. When he finished, he dismissed everyone back to work.

They had to get this boat out of here so they could continue with their itinerary. Even with everything that happened, their guests still needed to know they were the crew's number one priority. Love it or hate it, that was how things worked in this business.

Jimmy James helped Kenzie to her bunkroom so she could lie down. Then he knelt beside her and locked gazes with her. Emotion welled in his throat. He'd truly been afraid he was going to lose her again today.

"Kenzie . . ." He could hardly find the right words.

"I'm sorry." Her voice choked with emotion as she stared at him.

"I know you are. I'm just glad you're okay."

She wiped beneath her eyes as if tears had formed. "I know what you're thinking. You're thinking I should have never come on this boat."

He pressed his lips together as he considered his response. "I do worry that you're distracted by everything that's been happening. When you're on a boat like this, you can't afford to be preoccupied. It can mean life or death."

"I know. Believe me, I know."

He opened his mouth, wanting to tell her more. Wanting to let her know how much he cared about her. Wanting to ask her about those earrings and the real story behind why she'd taken them to that pawnshop.

Before he could, a knock sounded at the door. He glanced back and saw Roman standing there with a sheepish expression on his face.

"I know I'm not supposed to be down here, but I saw everything that happened, and I wanted to check on Kenzie. I hope I'm not overstepping . . ."

Jimmy James glanced at Kenzie, and she nodded, indicating that Roman could come in. Jimmy James would prefer the man didn't. Still, it wasn't his call.

Instead, he stood, rising to full height as he glanced at Roman. "Don't stay too long. She needs her rest."

Roman nodded and waited for Jimmy James to slip past before going inside.

But the fact that this guy was with Kenzie bothered Jimmy James entirely more than it should.

# CHAPTER THIRTY-TWO

"THAT LOOKED PRETTY SCARY," Roman said as he knelt on the floor beside Kenzie. "I know it's weird for guests to be down in the crew quarters. But I just really wanted to talk to you myself."

Kenzie appreciated his concern, even though it did surprise her. Having a guest down here was very unusual, to say the least. "Thank you. But I'm fine. Really."

"I felt like I was watching a movie or something. I didn't know stuff like that happened in real life. It was . . . something I'll never forget." He continued talking, almost as if this visit was about him and his reaction more than it was to check on Kenzie.

"Same here . . . the whole thing was surreal."

As he took a breath, his gaze drifted away from her eyes. "By the way, those are pretty earrings."

Instinctively, Kenzie touched one of them. "Thank you. They were my mom's."

"They're heirlooms? That's the best kind of jewelry."

"So, you do know a few things about jewelry . . ." Kenzie couldn't figure out who this guy really was. Was he cut from the same cloth as his family? Or did he and Kenzie really have things in common?

He shrugged at her statement. "When you grow up in a family like mine, you learn a few things about the business—whether you want to or not."

She sat up slightly as a new thought raced through her head—a thought that helped her forget about her throbbing ankle. "Do you know how to tell a real diamond from a fake one?"

He shrugged again. "My dad has shown me a few tips. Why?"

She raised a shoulder, trying to look casual. "For years, I thought these earrings were real. But I recently learned they weren't. But I know my dad wouldn't buy my mom fake diamond earrings."

Roman frowned and tilted his head. "Can I see one?"

Kenzie pulled one from her ear, and Roman held

it to the light. He squinted as he studied it, turning it and peering more closely.

"There are four Cs to determining the worth of a diamond," he said. "Color, clarity, cut, and carat."

"But what about determining a fake?"

He continued to study it. "There are tests for that also. Most experts look for small imperfections called inclusions."

"Real diamonds have imperfections?"

"They do, whereas lab-generated stones look perfect. Funny, huh?"

"It is surprising."

"There are other factors also. You can look at how the light reflects from the stone, check the hardness—although fakes can be pretty hard also—as well as buoyancy, fire resistance, and transparency."

A lot more went into the jewelry business than Kenzie ever realized. She waited while he continued to examine her stones.

"Someone did a very good job faking this." He handed it back to her. "But this is, indeed, fake."

She frowned. "Thanks for the confirmation."

"Jewelry is a surprisingly cutthroat business."

"Is it?" His statement caught Kenzie's interest. What did that mean? She knew so little about that business.

Roman touched the watch on his wrist. A Rolex? Quite possibly.

"Some pieces are worth a lot of money," he told her. "Like, *a lot* a lot of money."

"Your stepmom had some pretty fantastic-looking pieces."

Roman raised his eyebrows, as if ready to dish out any gossip Kenzie might even hint at being interested in. "Roselyn likes lots of bling, that's for sure. Some of the stuff she brought . . . it cost upward of a hundred thousand dollars."

"What?" Kenzie wasn't a jewelry girl herself, and she couldn't imagine someone wearing jewelry that expensive. She felt like she'd want to keep it locked away—which was one reason why she never wanted anything too expensive.

"She has even more costly pieces than that back at home. I guess jewelry makes her feel important. And she *loves* feeling important."

"I can't imagine traveling with anything that expensive."

"A yacht should be safe, right? It's not like it's a hotel. But Roselyn won't leave home without her jewelry. What good is it to have it if you don't flaunt it? That's her theory, not mine."

A better picture of the family formed in Kenzie's

mind. Some people needed others to know they were important.

Kind of like her stepmom, Leesa. That woman couldn't be any more different than Kenzie's mom. She still wasn't sure what her father saw in the woman.

Another question drifted into her mind. Since Roman was being chatty, maybe she could find out some more information. "How did your family even hear about *Almost Paradise*? Do you know?"

"As far as I know, the owner reaches out to certain people, offering them a deal as he gets his charter business established. I thought I heard my father say he even suggested going down to the jewelry show on the boat so we could arrive with style." Roman shrugged again, bitterness dripping from his words. "Whatever. I just figured a charter would be fun. I'm always up for fun."

"Of course." She had a feeling that would be his mantra for the rest of his life. This guy probably wouldn't ever have to work. Kenzie couldn't imagine being given that luxury, not that she would want it. She found working to be fulfilling.

Roman stood with a sigh and glanced down at her. "I suppose I should go now. You probably need your rest. But I look forward to hearing how you're doing tomorrow."

"Thanks, Roman." Kenzie watched him walk away.

Their conversation had been insightful.

But would it help her figure out who was targeting her?

Probably not.

She sank deeper into her bed at the thought.

---

JIMMY JAMES PACED THE BRIDGE. He couldn't get his mind off what happened with Kenzie earlier. She'd been only moments away from dying. From drowning. From a terrible, terrible death.

But he couldn't afford to make the same mistake Kenzie had. He couldn't afford to be distracted right now as they left Charleston. Their earlier departure had been delayed after Kenzie's accident.

Thirty minutes later, they were successfully heading south. If only they could head away from trouble so easily.

He wondered if Roman was still down with Kenzie and what they were talking about. He tried not to let insecurities get the best of him, but Jimmy

James couldn't stop thinking about the two of them alone together.

*Don't think like that*, he told himself.

But it was hard not to.

He heard a knock at the door behind him. His heart lifted as he wondered if it was Kenzie. Then he remembered she was injured and not exactly mobile right now.

He turned and saw Roselyn slink inside with a drink in her hand. The woman wore a bikini with a sheer black coverup on over it. Sunglasses perched atop her head, and her blonde hair had been smoothed into a twist.

He held back a frown as he braced himself for whatever this conversation might hold.

Having guests on the bridge was a bad idea. But Jimmy James had to maintain an air of hospitality also.

"I hope I'm not breaking any rules by coming in here," she murmured, stepping inside without an invitation.

"You're fine." He forced a polite smile.

Roselyn continued until she was at the helm, standing beside him. Her pungent perfume nearly took his breath away.

"I'm sorry to hear about what happened earlier,"

she started. "It's been all the talk of the boat. Is your steward okay?"

"She's going to be." Kenzie's image flashed in his mind, and he once again remembered how close he'd come to losing her. What would it take to keep her safe? What if he wasn't capable of doing that?

He didn't like that thought.

"That's good news." Roselyn took a sip of her champagne. "That had to be quite scary for her."

"It was scary for all of us. Thankfully, we have a happy ending."

"Yes, thankfully." She took another sip of her drink and stared out the window. She nodded toward Eddie, who was busy hosing off the deck. "That guy . . . he's your first mate, yes?"

"That's correct."

"Do you know what he did before this?"

"I can't say I do." Jimmy James had no idea where Roselyn was going with these questions. What he really wanted was a good reason to usher her out of here. "Why do you ask?"

"He looks familiar for some reason. Maybe he just has one of those faces."

Jimmy James stared at Eddie's angular, rather ordinary face and unremarkable features. He could see that. "Maybe."

She turned toward him and shrugged. "Either way, I just wanted to come up. I won't distract you too much."

"You have a good afternoon, Mrs. Abernathy."

"You too, Captain Gamble." She sashayed away.

As she did, Jimmy James glanced at Eddie one more time.

Was someone on this boat responsible for what had been happening?

He didn't know, but he didn't like the thought of it.

# CHAPTER THIRTY-THREE

KENZIE WAS EXHAUSTED. Her adrenaline had worn off, and now all she wanted to do was sleep.

But her ankle hurt too much.

Even though she'd taken a pain reliever, the medicine hadn't begun to touch her discomfort yet.

One of the worst things she could do for her mental health was to lie in bed doing nothing.

Doing so gave her too much time to think. To replay the events of the past several days. To let questions repeat over and over in her head.

Why had Sunni asked her to get that cooler when she did? Was it a coincidence?

Kenzie wanted to think that it was. But it was clear that someone on the boat might want her dead.

Could that person be Sunni? Was that her way of trying to get rid of Kenzie for good? Or had it just been an honest mistake?

And what about Kenzie's earrings? She had a hard time believing those diamonds had always been fake. But what other option was there?

She had too many questions and not enough answers.

In the middle of all her questions, her phone rang.

She looked at the screen and frowned.

Leesa's name showed.

The woman seemed to want to get rid of Kenzie so she could have Kenzie's father all to herself. At least, that's how it felt.

Why would Leesa be calling now? Leesa *never* called Kenzie.

Kenzie stared at the screen, considering not answering. But finally, on the fifth ring, she did—mostly out of curiosity.

"Kenzie . . ." Leesa's icy cold voice came through the line. "I'm sorry to disturb you. But it's important."

Something about the way Leesa said the words made Kenzie's back muscles tighten. "What is it?"

"Have you seen your father?"

"Not since last week. Why?"

"He's not answering his phone. I wondered if he went to Lantern Beach to try to talk some sense into you again."

The tension in her shoulders deepened. "He hasn't. Maybe he's in surgery."

"He's not."

"Did he go to the mountain cabin?" Kenzie's mind raced through possible scenarios. "He likes to go there to think, and the phone service in that region is horrible."

"He didn't mention it. We weren't exactly on speaking terms last I saw him. But he's never left in anger and refused to talk to me for this long before. He's much more level-headed than that."

Kenzie wondered what their fight had been about, but she didn't ask. She had a feeling it was her. That seemed to be the pattern she'd seen.

"If Dad came down to see me, he would tell you. Right? I mean, that's a long trip to take and not mention it."

"Not necessarily." Leesa let out a sigh. "He probably knows I wouldn't approve."

"Of course, you wouldn't," Kenzie muttered before she could stop herself.

"What's that supposed to mean?"

"Nothing." Kenzie knew better than to get into an argument now. "I haven't seen my father. I'm actually on a boat out in the ocean right now."

Leesa let out a long sigh. "If you hear from him, can you let me know?"

"I will. I'm sure you'll get up with him soon though."

At the end of the call, a moment of doubt hit Kenzie. Was something wrong with her dad?

No, that was ridiculous. Just because someone didn't answer the phone the moment it rang didn't mean something was wrong.

At least, Kenzie hoped that was the case.

---

AS JIMMY JAMES walked onto the deck, he spotted Owen in the distance. He glanced around and noted that no one else was nearby. Maybe this would be the perfect time to talk to his deckhand.

"Owen," he called as he stepped closer.

"Yes, Captain?" Owen paused from covering a piece of deck furniture.

"I have something I need to talk to you about. Is this a good time?"

"Yes, Captain. What's going on?"

Jimmy James paused as he considered how to approach the subject. Finally, he decided to simply dive in. "As you know, there have been some strange things happening lately. Is there anything you want to tell me about your connection to any of those events?"

Owen sucked in a breath before quickly shaking his head. "No, sir. Is there a reason why you're asking?"

"Right before the marina fire, someone said they saw you near the boat that was involved. Is that true?"

He took a step back and raised his hands, his defenses clearly rising. "I *was* at the marina. I went out to my car to get something, but I was already on *Almost Paradise* when I saw the fire break out. I didn't have anything to do with it."

"What about the white gloves in the back of the dresser you share with Eddie? Can you explain those?"

"In my drawer? What are you talking about?" Owen's voice lilted with surprise.

"When Mrs. Abernathy's necklace disappeared, I searched the crew's quarters. I found some white gloves—they reminded me of something a magician might wear during a show. Seemed like an odd thing to bring on the boat with you considering the limited space."

"I stuffed all my things in the drawers. If there are white gloves on the boat, then maybe whoever used that drawer before me left them there. Because I'm certainly no magician. I have no use for white gloves."

Jimmy James wasn't ready to concede yet. "What about the towline incident that happened today? Did you have anything to do with that? Certainly, you saw Kenzie heading that way and could have stopped her."

Owen's shoulders sagged, and he leaned against the railing as if defeated. "Look, I don't know where all this is coming from. But I like Kenzie. I yelled when I saw her coming. There's no way I'd ask anyone to go near a coil of rope as we're departing. Her foot could have been severed. I wouldn't purposefully put anyone in that position. Do you seriously think someone is targeting Kenzie with that kind of vengeance?"

Jimmy James finally settled on saying, "I'm just trying to get to the bottom of what's going on. All these events appear to be centered not only around Kenzie, but on this boat. That's unacceptable."

"I agree. I don't like the sound of that either. But I'm not involved. I can promise you that."

Jimmy James crossed his arms over his broad chest. "Do you have any idea who might be?"

"What do you mean? Do you think someone I know might be involved?"

"That's my best guess at this point."

Owen adamantly shook his head. "No one I know could be involved in this. I don't even want to think about that being a possibility. The marina fire? There's no reason to think this boat was connected. The gloves in the drawer? Like I said, probably just a leftover from some past crew member. The towline incident? As far as I'm concerned, that was just an accident."

Jimmy James stared at him another moment, trying to get at the truth in his gaze. Finally, he nodded. "Very well. Go back to work then."

But as Jimmy James headed back to the bridge to take over from Eddie, he still felt unsettled. He had too many unanswered questions—and they weren't just the ones he'd posed to Owen.

Why was Kenzie in a pawnshop? Had Kenzie

and Roman really bonded so much that Roman felt the need to come down to the crew quarters to check on her?

Jimmy James didn't know what was going on aboard this boat, but he didn't like it.

# CHAPTER THIRTY-FOUR

KENZIE'S ANKLE still hurt the next morning, but she kept it wrapped with ice all she could. She knew from a quick visit with Araminta that they were already underway toward St. Augustine.

By water, it was approximately four hours before they got there. However, they wouldn't be disembarking this evening. Instead, once the boat was docked, the Abernathys wanted to have a diamond themed Putting on the Glitz dinner party and invite eight friends aboard the boat to celebrate with them. Their friends would depart after the party and return to their own accommodations onshore.

Kenzie felt terrible that Sunni and Araminta would have to carry the extra workload during the celebration. But there was little Kenzie could do about it with her ankle injured like it was.

Besides, she couldn't stop thinking about that conversation she had with Leesa last night. Certainly, her dad was okay. He wasn't answering his phone simply because he was at the mountain cabin where there was no cell service. It was the only thing that made sense.

Still, Kenzie didn't like this.

Shortly after nine a.m., Kenzie decided she couldn't stay in bed anymore. She would get cleaned up and grab a bite to eat in the crew mess.

She stood from her bed, trying not to flinch as pain throbbed at her ankle.

Instead, she hobbled toward the door. Before she reached it, voices drifted from the hallway. Sunni and Araminta were talking.

"As soon as this charter's over, I'm going to find a way to go on a date with Captain Gamble."

"I don't think so," Sunni said. "I think he and Kenzie like each other."

"You mean, *Kenzie* likes Captain Gamble."

"What do you mean?"

"I mean, I'm totally more his type than she is. Guys like Captain Gamble get bored with girls like

Kenzie. She's so *vanilla*." Vanilla was spoken as if it were a bad word.

"No one's going to argue that the two of them are totally different."

"It's more than that," Araminta continued. "I see the way he looks at me. He's interested. I'm way more fun."

"Do you think?" Sunni asked.

"I *definitely* think."

Sunni chuckled. "Right now, I need you to check the galley to see how breakfast is coming. I'll be up in a moment to help you. I'm going to check on Kenzie first."

"Have fun."

Kenzie lowered herself on the edge of the bed, wishing she hadn't overheard that conversation. It was too late to erase it from her mind now. Araminta might have a point about Kenzie and Jimmy James. The two of them were definitely mismatched. But, in Kenzie's opinion, that's what made them work. Besides, she'd never felt a connection with someone like she did Jimmy James.

Before Kenzie had time to compose herself, someone knocked at the door. After she called, "Come in!" Sunni appeared with a bright smile on her face, acting as if that whole conversation hadn't just happened.

"How are you doing?" she asked.

Kenzie shrugged, not especially wanting to be fake. "I've been better."

Sunni's smile quickly faded as her gaze clouded. "Look, Kenzie. I just want to say I'm sorry for sending you down yesterday to grab that cooler. If I had had any idea what was going to happen . . ."

"There was no way you could have known."

"I should have known better. I knew we were about to depart. I just thought you had time. . ."

She stared at Sunni. The woman looked honestly apologetic. But Kenzie still reminded herself to keep the woman at arm's length.

If Sunni were truly her friend, she wouldn't have been talking to Araminta about Jimmy James and giggling about Kenzie being "vanilla."

Instead of bringing that up, Kenzie said, "What's done is done. And, thankfully, my ankle will be okay."

"Do you need anything?"

"I'm good. I'm just going to lie down."

"Call me if you need anything, and I'll do my best to help. Okay?"

Kenzie nodded. "Okay then."

She was going to have to try her best not to stew over what she'd heard.

Besides, she had bigger things to worry about.

AFTER BREAKFAST WAS OVER, Jimmy James headed down to Kenzie's room to check on her. He would pay the same courtesy to any of his crew members who'd been injured.

He tried to wait until a little later in case she was sleeping.

Plus, he had to admit part of him wanted to hold back.

The reaction was probably a mix of things. Seeing her with Roman. Wondering what kind of secrets she was hiding after that trip to the pawnshop. Maybe even a few remnants of his conversation with Kenzie's dad still haunted him, even though he thought he had put that behind him.

Either way, relationships were complicated. They were even more complicated working on a boat like this. Adding to that was the vast difference in his and Kenzie's backgrounds.

Was he a fool to think that something between them could work?

If he'd asked himself that a few days ago, the answer would have been no. But now he felt uncertain.

Shoving those doubts aside, he knocked on the door and heard Kenzie mumble for him to come in. He pushed the door open and saw Kenzie lying on her back, staring at the bunk above her.

He stepped inside farther and closed the door. Then lowered himself on the edge of the bed to get a good look at her.

Seeing Kenzie dispelled his doubts. When Jimmy James was with her, that happened—and she didn't even have to say a word. The strength of her character and spirit spoke for her.

"How are you?" he asked quietly.

She sighed and ran a hand through her hair, appearing as if she was at wit's end. Her skin looked pale, her hair rumpled, and her eyes had lost their glow. "I don't know anymore."

That wasn't the answer he wanted to hear. But her physical pain mixed with the emotional trauma of everything that had happened was clearly taking a toll on her.

"Can I see your ankle?" he asked.

"Sure."

Jimmy James scooted down farther and removed the ice pack from near her foot. Gently, he touched the skin around her ankle, trying to see if the swelling had gone down. The area didn't look quite as puffy as it had earlier.

"It's looking a little better," he murmured. "Does it hurt any less?"

She shook her head. "Unfortunately, no. I just took another Tylenol, though."

Jimmy James stared at her, so many things on his mind that he wanted to talk to her about. But right now, Kenzie needed to concentrate on getting better. Worrying about the strange and mysterious incidents happening should be left to him.

Jimmy James grabbed her hand and squeezed it. "Is there anything I can do for you?"

"No, there's not. But thank you for coming to check on me."

"Of course." Jimmy James kissed the top of her hand before standing. "I'll be back later. Radio me if you need anything."

"I will."

As soon as he left the room, he didn't feel any better than he did when he went in.

But it could be worse. He could be trying to

contact her father right now to let him know his daughter was dead.

He praised God that wasn't the case.

# CHAPTER THIRTY-FIVE

AS KENZIE KILLED MORE time in her bunkroom, she grabbed her computer. She rested it on her abdomen before typing in Mr. Robertson's name and waiting to see what popped up.

She knew the man was quirky and owned several businesses. Apparently, the dot-com boom had been where he made a lot of his money. At least, that's what Kenzie had understood from Eddie.

To her surprise, she didn't find anything about the man online.

Was that because he was private? Or was there something more to it?

Maybe that idea was ridiculous. Maybe she was simply reading too much into this whole situation.

Not every millionaire wanted his face plastered out there.

Still, she did think it was curious. Why couldn't she find anything out about the man online? Not even a picture showing how he looked?

She supposed it didn't matter.

She closed her computer, but questions still raced through her mind. Her theory remained that the person behind these crimes against her was on the boat. At least, one of them was. The text message she got made it clear that more than one person was involved.

She nibbled on her bottom lip and thought for a moment. As she did, her phone buzzed.

She glanced at the screen and saw that someone had sent her a picture. Instantly, her guard went up.

As she clicked on the photo, she saw that it had been taken from a distance. It was of her dad sitting on the porch at the mountain cabin that he owned.

He looked oblivious that anybody was nearby.

Concern rushed through her.

This was a threat. Someone wanted to let Kenzie know that they had her dad in their sights.

She quickly closed the picture. She needed to tell someone what was going on. Even though they were in Florida and out of Cassidy's jurisdiction, the police chief was the only law enforcement official Kenzie trusted with this information.

She prayed her new friend would know how to handle this situation.

---

JIMMY JAMES LET Eddie take over at the helm after Kenzie called him on the radio. He rushed to her room, anxious to know what was going on. When he walked into the space, he saw her sitting up in bed. Her face appeared even more ashen than it had earlier as she twirled the earring in her ear.

"You're supposed to have that ankle iced." He pointed to her leg.

She shrugged, that frozen look remaining on her face. "I know. But this is more important."

He sat beside her on the bed and glanced at the phone she clutched in her free hand. "What's going on?"

Kenzie told him about the conversation she'd had with Leesa, as well as the picture she'd received of her father.

A new rush of concern filled Jimmy James. "There was no message with the picture?"

"There was nothing. No threat or mention of 'do

this or else.' It was just a photo. Someone clearly wants to keep me on edge. I already called Cassidy and told her about it. She's going to get someone to the cabin to check on my dad."

"How about Leesa? Did you call her after you got the text?"

Kenzie pressed her lips together quickly before nodding. "I did. I didn't tell her everything, just that I thought my father could be at the cabin."

Jimmy James rubbed his jaw as he processed the new information. "Someone doesn't want you to forget that you're a target. Now they're going after your dad to get to you."

Kenzie pressed her eyes shut, her neck appearing corded with tension. "I know. I don't know what to do about it. I never guessed these people would get my dad involved. They must have been following him." Her eyes popped back open and latched onto Jimmy James'. "What should I do?"

His mind raced through the possibilities until one stood out from the rest. "I think that you should text this guy who threatened you earlier and ask him what he wants."

She sucked in a quick breath. "You think I should engage?"

"I do. But there's more to this. Before you send

this text, I'll go onto the bridge where the security camera feed is set up. I want to see if any of our crew members glance at their phones when they receive a message."

Kenzie's eyes widened. "Because you think that text could have been sent by someone on the crew . . ."

"There's a good possibility someone on this crew is working with someone else not on this boat."

"I've thought the same thing." She pressed her lips together before asking, "You really think this could work?"

"That's the only thing I can think of to do right now. Everyone's getting ready for the party tonight. Maybe this will give us some of the answers we need." He rose and took a step toward the door.

Kenzie stood and wobbled before gaining her balance. "I want to go with you. Please."

Jimmy James stared at her another moment, wishing she wasn't involved in this. But she already was, whether she wanted to be or not. Trying to keep her locked away somewhere safe wasn't going to work.

He offered a resolute nod. "I'll help you upstairs then."

# CHAPTER THIRTY-SIX

KENZIE FELT apprehension rush through her at the possible implications of what they were about to do. But along with that apprehension was a touch of hope as well. Maybe—just maybe—this would provide them with some answers they needed.

Jimmy James helped her up the steps onto the bridge. He dismissed Eddie before leading Kenzie inside. He then opened the sliding door where the security monitors were kept. The cameras were only in common areas, so any crew members or guests in their quarters couldn't be seen.

But it was like Jimmy James said—everyone was busy getting ready for the party tonight, so the crew scurried about the boat.

In fact, each crew member appeared to be accounted for on the screens.

Jimmy James and Kenzie glanced at each other as they stood staring at the monitors. Jimmy James gave her an affirmative nod to signal she could send her message to the person who'd texted her earlier.

With trembling hands, Kenzie took her phone out and typed her reply.

WHAT DO **you want from me?**

HER FINGER HOVERED over the Send button for only a moment until she pressed it. The *swooping* sound made it clear the message had gone through.

Now she just had to wait.

She and Jimmy James stared at the security screens, watching to see if anyone would grab his or her phone after hearing a buzz or beep to indicate a new message.

Which crew member could be behind this?

Kenzie didn't want to think any of them could be involved. But she didn't want to be naive either.

She waited. Held her breath. Hoped to see some kind of indication as to who was involved.

But none of the crew members touched their phones.

She frowned. "Maybe this was too much of a long shot."

"Maybe. But let's wait a little longer."

As soon as Jimmy James said the words, Kenzie's breath caught. She pointed at a different screen. "He just grabbed his phone and is checking something on the screen."

She and Jimmy James leaned closer.

The problem was that it wasn't a crew member who'd checked their phone.

It was Roman Abernathy.

———

JIMMY JAMES SAT DOWN and rubbed his jaw in thought as he stared at the screen. Roman had glanced at his phone, but then he put it away and continued playing pool. It could be a coincidence. Bad timing.

But maybe it wasn't.

"What are we going to do now?" Kenzie lowered herself into the seat beside him.

"I'm not sure I can, in good conscience, confront a guest. Plus, I have a hard time seeing how Roman

Abernathy might be involved in this. Why would he possibly want to target you?"

"I have no idea why *anyone* would want to target me. I guess until we know the why, it's going to be harder for us to know who."

"You're probably right." Jimmy James leaned back and stared at the screen.

Roman continued to play a game of pool with his family. If he was concerned about anything, he certainly didn't show it. Could Roman be behind something like this? He had a hard time seeing it.

Unless maybe he wanted to prove something to his family. To somehow make his own money—even if the means to obtain it were illegal. If that were the case, who did he have helping him? Who was watching Kenzie's dad?

He didn't even have any good guesses.

Jimmy James glanced at Kenzie again, watching her expression to see if anything had changed. "I don't suppose you've gotten any response yet."

Kenzie look down at her phone and frowned. Her voice quivered as she said, "No, nothing yet. I hope my dad . . ."

Jimmy James scooted closer and pulled her into a gentle hug. As he did, Kenzie leaned into his chest but didn't cry. Still, he could feel the tension coming from her.

"Chief Chambers will get someone to check on your father," he murmured into her soft hair. "Maybe this is just an empty threat."

"Maybe. But nothing makes sense."

"I agree." He tightened his arms around her. "This is all confusing."

"I don't even know what to do, Jimmy James. I feel totally clueless right now."

He kissed the top of her head. "We'll figure it out. Together."

# CHAPTER THIRTY-SEVEN

JIMMY JAMES CALLED Eddie back to the helm so he could help Kenzie to her room. As soon as they left the bridge, they nearly collided with Roman.

Kenzie stiffened as she remembered seeing the security footage of him checking his phone after she'd sent that text. But she couldn't let his presence shake her up. It was hard not to, considering everything at stake.

"Kenzie." Roman warmly glanced down toward her foot. "How's your ankle today?"

She offered a feeble smile as she remembered her near-death experience. "It's a little better."

"That's good news. Usually everything feels worse on the second day."

"I'm just trying to push through."

"Don't push too hard. Rest is probably the best thing you can do in this situation." He leaned closer as if sharing a secret. "Even if my family starts complaining about lack of service, don't listen to them. They think the world revolves around them."

Kenzie smiled. She wanted to like this guy. She really did. At least Roman viewed his social standing with a touch of humor.

But as she remembered him glancing at his phone, she realized just how hard it was for her to trust anyone. Someone on this boat was hiding something and wanted her dead. She couldn't afford to let down her guard.

She and Jimmy James continued past Roman toward the stairway.

Jimmy James waited until Kenzie was situated in her bed with fresh ice on her ankle before he left. But she saw the worry in his gaze.

He didn't like what was going on any more than she did.

But the worst part for Kenzie was knowing that she could only lie here, waiting to see if anything else happened.

JIMMY JAMES WENT BACK to the bridge and relieved Eddie from his post. But his mind raced through each and every development.

When Stevie-o called him, it was a welcome relief from his otherwise heavy thoughts. Jimmy James quickly answered and put the device on speaker.

"Hey, man," Jimmy James said. "What's going on?"

"I just thought I'd give you an update."

"Did you sign the paperwork?" Jimmy James tried to keep the touch of sourness from his voice, but he didn't like the idea of the marina being sold.

"As a matter of fact . . . I didn't. I changed my mind."

Jimmy James straightened. "What? I thought the offer was too good to refuse."

"Maybe. But what am I going to do if I don't work here? Even if I did make some money on the sale, knowing my wife, she'll just spend it. I'm better off staying busy."

Stevie-o's wife had a spending problem that had gotten the couple into some serious debt.

"I didn't think you should sell, but I didn't want to say anything," Jimmy James said. "How did Murphy handle the news?"

"Not well. At first, he tried to convince me otherwise. He even upped his offer some. But I still said no. That's when his personality switched, and he became irate."

Jimmy James could totally picture that. "What did he say?"

"He said he'd ruin me. That if I wasn't going to sell this place to him, that he'd find another way to get it."

Jimmy James' back muscles bristled. "What?"

"I know. Can you believe that guy would say something like that? Actually, I can. He seems just like the type who gets what he wants."

"Does that make you nervous? Did it make you reconsider?"

"There's no way." Stevie-o's voice hardened. "Hearing him talk like that made my resolve strengthen even more."

"Good for you. But keep your eyes out for trouble, just in case."

"Don't worry. I will. I just thought I'd give you that update."

Jimmy James thanked his friend before ending the call.

At least, that was settled.

But from the sound of it, Murphy Bassett might be sticking around to cause more trouble. That was the last thing they needed, especially considering everything else that had been going on lately.

# CHAPTER THIRTY-EIGHT

FOUR HOURS LATER, Kenzie simply couldn't lie in bed anymore. She knew she couldn't do much to help the rest of the crew, but she needed to do something.

She hobbled up the steps and into the galley. Everyone tried to shoo her back downstairs, but she wouldn't listen.

Instead, she helped the stews by polishing some silverware, ensuring no fingerprints were on the glasses, and washing a few dishes for Chef Durango.

Ten minutes before the party started—once all her work was done—she stepped onto the aft deck where the event would take place and saw the area had been decorated. Clear crystals that resembled diamonds hung on the edges of the space. Black and gold balloons formed an archway near the door. Even the ice cubes were shaped like diamonds for the event.

Sunni had done a good job transforming the place.

In the distance, she saw Jimmy James dressed in a black tux readying himself to greet everyone at tonight's event. The sight of him made her throat go dry. He looked dashing, like he'd worn clothes like that a million times before. No one would guess he was more comfortable in boat shoes and T-shirts.

She felt her cheeks flush and looked away. This was no time to gawk . . . but she'd be perfectly content to stare at him for the rest of the evening and dream about the future.

Instead, Kenzie watched as Abernathys trickled from their rooms in time to greet their friends. A few minutes later, they were all seated at the table, ready for their appetizers. Everyone had dressed to the nines, as the saying went. A string quartet played eloquent melodies in the distance.

What she noticed most was the jewelry each guest wore. Every piece was extravagant and screamed *look at me*.

Then again, the only reason the Abernathys had

invited their friends on this boat was to, as Roman called it, flex and flaunt their wealth.

Serving this many people and only having one chef would be challenging, especially since the crew was down a person. The good news was that the deckhands were also pitching in to help with service.

Sunni and Araminta served appetizers. Mini beef tourtieres, honey-mint lamb skewers, and shrimp tartlets. The scent of each dish wafted in the air until Kenzie's stomach rumbled. Chef Durango had really outdone himself.

Everything was going well until the main dish was served.

That's when Mrs. Abernathy gasped, and her hand went to her throat.

Kenzie braced herself, expecting bad news—an allergic reaction, food lodged in her throat, maybe even a bee sting.

Instead, Roselyn raised her hand and displayed something sparkly inside.

"The *diamond* just *fell* out of my *necklace*. How did that even happen?"

Mr. Abernathy rose and stepped toward her, his brow wrinkled with concern. "What? That should never happen, not with my jewelry."

Roselyn held up the princess-cut diamond, which was probably three carats.

"Well, it did. This is just embarrassing." Her words rang with accusation.

"Don't look at me like it's my fault." Mr. Abernathy narrowed his eyes, clearly put off by his wife's reaction.

Roselyn's nostrils flared. "Aren't you the one who gave this to me?"

"Maybe you're not taking care of it," he shot back.

Mrs. Abernathy was clearly embarrassed by her broken necklace, but not at all embarrassed by her own behavior.

Kenzie felt a headache coming on.

Maybe she should lie back down before their argument got any louder and made her headache worse.

Still, she'd never forget the sight of Mrs. Abernathy holding that huge precious gemstone in her hands.

Why had that stone fallen out?

JIMMY JAMES LISTENED to the argument as he sat at the head of the table. Mr. and Mrs. Abernathy had most likely had too much to drink. Alcohol only exacerbated situations like these.

He wished he was anywhere but here, that he could slip away like Kenzie had.

"Captain, may I have a word with you?" Roman appeared beside him.

Jimmy James' back muscles tensed, but he nodded to everyone at the table and excused himself. He and Roman walked into the main salon, and Jimmy James waited to hear what was on his guest's mind.

"Listen, I went to the bathroom a few minutes ago." Roman kept his voice low. "But I stopped in the master stateroom to look at some of Roselyn's necklaces."

"Why would you do that?" Jimmy James crossed his arms, apprehensive about where this talk was going.

"I was thinking about a conversation I had yesterday with Kenzie—about how she discovered the diamonds in her heirloom earrings weren't real. There's no way that diamond should have fallen out of Roselyn's necklace. I know the craftsmanship behind it. It's good."

"So, what are you saying?"

"It got me to wondering. If Kenzie's diamonds aren't real, what about Roselyn's? So, I examined some of her jewelry."

"And?"

"I don't think her gemstones are real."

Jimmy James stiffened at his words. "I'm not really sure what you're getting at. Did your stepmom bring fake jewelry on the boat?"

Roman shrugged. "That's just the thing. I don't think she did. She's not the type."

Jimmy James took a moment to let that sink in. "Do you think the jewelry has been switched out for replicas?"

"I don't know. That's why I wanted to tell you. I'm not bringing this up to my dad. Not until I know something more."

Jimmy James raised his head. "Thank you. I'm going to think this through before I ask any questions. If you would, let's keep this between us for now. If something is going on, I don't want to put anyone in danger."

"Understood."

A creak sounded behind them. Jimmy James turned but saw no one.

Had someone overheard their conversation?

He quickly strode toward the doorway and peered beyond it.

No one was there.

Maybe he was just being paranoid.

He hoped that was the case. Because if the wrong person had just overheard what Roman had told him . . .

As he and Roman walked back out to the deck to finish their meal, Jimmy James' thoughts raced.

Was this precarious situation somehow linked to jewelry?

He didn't know. But if he wanted to keep Kenzie safe, he needed to do some quick research.

# CHAPTER THIRTY-NINE

KENZIE AWOKE the next morning to a text message from Jimmy James asking her to meet him on the bridge as soon as she woke. He offered to help her get upstairs if she needed assistance.

She glanced at the time on her phone and saw it was only 5:30 a.m. Probably no one else was up yet—except Jimmy James, who'd just sent the message.

She stood, putting weight on her ankle. It still throbbed, but not quite as badly. She took another pain reliever to help get her through the next several hours. Then she got dressed, her curiosity racing. If Jimmy James wanted to talk to her, then he had a good reason.

Kenzie slipped onto the bridge and saw Jimmy

James sitting with coffee in hand and a pensive look on his face.

She cleared her throat. "Good morning."

A thin smile crossed his lips as he turned to her. "Kenzie. Good morning. I hope I didn't wake you."

"You didn't. I was having trouble sleeping. What's going on?"

"Have a seat. Take some weight off your ankle." He ushered her to a seat and made sure her leg was elevated.

"What's going on, Jimmy James?" she asked. "I know that's not why you asked me to come here."

Was this about the strange events that had happened? Or was it about the two of them?

Had their relationship somehow reached a tipping point? Had Jimmy James realized someone like Araminta really was a better fit for his future?

Insecurity tried to strangle her, but she pushed it away.

He frowned and rubbed his jaw. "Roman said something to me last night that stayed on my mind. I wanted to give myself some time to think it over before I told you."

Kenzie leaned back, suddenly feeling unsteady. But at least this conversation wasn't about the two of them. "You're making me nervous."

"I'm sorry. I'm not trying to do that. It's just that . . ." He shook his head before looking outside at the darkness surrounding them. Then he lowered his voice. "Roman believes some of his stepmother's real jewelry has been switched out for replicas."

Kenzie baulked. "What? What sense does that make?"

"That's what I'm trying to figure out. You were there last night when the diamond fell from her necklace. Roman said that's not normal, that there's no way his father didn't fully inspect that necklace before he gave it to his wife."

"Okay . . ." Kenzie's mind raced as she tried to connect all the dots.

"He believes that the diamond is fake. A very good fake."

She sucked in a breath. "Really? But . . ."

"The diamonds in your earrings were also fake."

The truth tried to settle on her, but part of Kenzie rebelled. Part of her didn't want to believe the conclusions that formed in her mind.

"Do you think someone on this boat is taking jewelry and replacing the real thing for fakes?" she finally asked.

Jimmy James crossed his arms and leaned back. "That's my theory. Almost every charter guest who's come on this boat has had some type of expensive jewelry they've brought with them. Right?"

Kenzie thought back through all the guests and nodded. "Yes, that's correct. And my earrings as well . . ."

His face darkened. "I think someone on this boat has ulterior motives. I think they could be wrapped up in a scheme that probably makes them millions of dollars as they swap out real jewelry for high-quality replicas."

"Wow . . . I don't even know what to say." She raked a hand through her hair.

"I know. Believe me. I almost didn't even want to tell you because it sounds so crazy."

Her mind continued to race. "But who would be skilled enough to do something like that? And it seems like that would take weeks to implement. The turnaround time is too quick."

"Maybe one of our crew members has some secret skills. Whoever is responsible is clearly working with someone else outside the boat as well. I agree with you about the timeline. But maybe someone has figured out a way to make this work."

"Jimmy James . . . what are we going to do with this information?"

"That's what I'm trying to figure out. I wanted to run this past you first before I made any calls."

"I don't want your theory to make sense, but it does. We have to tell someone."

He nodded almost grimly. "I'm going to call Chief Chambers and get her feedback."

As he said the words, Kenzie's phone beeped, and she glanced down and felt a new thread of tension wind through her.

"I have another message," she muttered. "It's from the same number that sent me that picture of my dad yesterday."

Jimmy James moved to sit beside her and leaned close to her. "What does it say?"

"It's a picture of my dad stepping out the door at his cabin, looking totally clueless anyone is watching him. It says: do exactly as I say or your father will die."

---

AS JIMMY JAMES read the words on Kenzie's phone one more time, his hands fisted at his sides.

Kenzie looked up at him, her eyes wide and almost childlike with fear. "What are we going to do?"

He swallowed hard before answering. "Whoever is behind this clearly knows we're catching on to what's happening. We have to keep this between you and me. I'll call Cassidy, but nobody else can know. We don't confront anybody or make any sudden moves."

"Makes sense."

The next instant, another picture appeared on her phone. This time it was of a box at the front door of the cabin. The text read, "Tick, tick, tick."

A soft cry escaped her lips. "Dad . . ."

Jimmy James slipped an arm around her waist as he looked at her phone and let out a grunt. "Did you ever hear anything from Chief Chambers about him? Did she get someone to go check on him?"

Kenzie shook her head. "Cassidy actually called last night and told me that some officers had gone past the cabin, but my dad wasn't there. What sense does that make? This is clearly a picture of him."

"But we don't know when it was taken or what kind of games these people are playing."

"What if they have my dad?" Her voice trembled.

Jimmy James pulled her toward him for another hug, unable to understand the complete agony she had to be feeling.

As her phone buzzed a third time, they both leaned together to read the message.

ONCE YOUR GUESTS are off the boat, figure out a way to get rid of the crew. We need to talk. Tell anyone and your father will die. Don't test me.

"OH, JIMMY JAMES . . ."

He pulled his arms more tightly around her.

"I don't know what this person is planning. But let's tell Cassidy what's going on. Then we need to pretend like we're playing by his rules."

# CHAPTER FORTY

KENZIE COULD HARDLY CONTROL the nerves raking through her.

What was the person behind this planning? What if there wasn't a solution to this? Someone had already tried to kill her twice. Would they succeed this time?

Kenzie and Jimmy James had called Cassidy and given her the update. She was working behind the scenes to help them.

But she was also more than five hundred miles away.

Right at eight, the crew lined up to bid goodbye to the Abernathys as they departed for their jewelry show. Once their luggage had been unloaded and they were gone, Jimmy James turned to the crew. His expression looked grim—he had lines around his eyes, tight lips, and stiff shoulders.

Kenzie knew why.

This situation was taking a toll on him as well.

"I know we normally have a tip meeting and clean the boat right after the guests depart," he started. "But you've all been working so hard that I'm going to give you some time off to enjoy St. Augustine. Go out, explore, grab a bite to eat. Then let's meet back here in a few hours, and we'll get some work done. Sound good?"

"Are you going to come too?" Araminta blinked at him, as if hopeful the two of them might spend some time together.

Kenzie wanted to roll her eyes, but she didn't. She didn't have time to be jealous—or even irritated. All she could think about right now was survival.

"I'm going to stay here and get some paperwork done," Jimmy James announced.

"Are you sure you don't want to come?" Araminta tilted her head, an almost whiny tone to her voice.

"I'm sure. But, please, go enjoy yourself."

Araminta stared at Jimmy James another minute as if contemplating the best way to manipulate him into coming. But Jimmy James cut her off before she could say anything else.

"Enough standing around here talking," he announced. "Go. Have fun. Before I change my mind."

The crew changed out of their whites into more casual clothing and then departed, leaving only Kenzie and Jimmy James onboard.

Neither of them said anything to each other as they quietly waited in the main salon—not until the last crew member had gone.

"What now?" Kenzie rushed as she glanced up at him.

"My best guess is that you'll get another message with instructions."

"I'm so anxious right now that I feel like I could throw up." She rubbed her arms.

Jimmy James stepped closer and stooped down to meet her gaze. "I know, and I'm sorry. I'd say you could leave the boat too. But I have a feeling whoever's behind this is watching us, and I know you don't want to put your father in jeopardy."

"I'll never forgive myself if he's hurt because of me."

Just as she said the words, footsteps sounded

behind them. She turned and saw Eddie enter the salon.

"I just realized I forgot my wallet and came back to get it." Eddie's gaze shifted suspiciously between Jimmy James and Kenzie. "You're not going to go enjoy St. Augustine, Kenzie?"

"Not with my ankle. I'll just rest here."

"Is everything okay?" Eddie continued.

"It's fine," Jimmy James said. "Grab your wallet and have some fun before all your time is wasted."

Eddie nodded, still giving them a curious look.

A few minutes later, he rushed up the stairs and ran by, holding up his wallet as he did so. Kenzie watched as he disappeared from sight.

Her heart thumped in her chest, the anticipation of the unknown almost more than she could bear.

When was this guy going to message her again? Did he have her dad? Was her dad okay?

There were too many unknowns for her comfort right now.

Just as the thought went through her head, her phone buzzed. She braced herself as she looked down at the message.

THE MESSAGE HAD READ: Go down into the engine room.

Jimmy James realized Kenzie had little choice but to do as this person had asked. He'd be right by her side when she did. But if push came to shove, he would fight with everything he had to protect her.

With one hand on Kenzie's back, they walked down the steps together.

He knew it wasn't out of the question that someone could have boarded the boat from one of the lower decks.

When they reached the engine room, a man stepped out from behind the boat's sewage plant.

Kenzie gasped beside him. "You? Murphy Bassett?"

Jimmy James shook his head as he observed the man, the guy who'd wanted to buy the marina.

The man smirked. "You can call me Mr. Robertson."

The breath left Jimmy James' lungs. He hadn't seen that one coming. "*You're* Mr. Robertson?"

"Murphy Bassett's my real name. I just go by Mr. Robertson just to keep things simple."

"I guess that explains why you have no online presence," Kenzie muttered.

"Smart girl. You looked into it, huh? However, all those smarts are exactly what's getting you in trouble right now."

She bristled. "What do you mean?"

"I mean, I thought you'd turn a blind eye to anything happening here on the boat. But you didn't. That's when I knew I had to get rid of you."

"Get rid of me so you could continue with your operation?" Kenzie's voice trembled.

"That's right. Captain Bridgemore was originally in on this. But we all know what happened to him. He tried to do more than one deal. He apparently wanted to do whatever he could to make money, and that didn't turn out well for him. Unfortunately, your curiosity isn't going to turn out well for you either."

Kenzie took a step back. "You don't have to do this."

"Unfortunately, I do. I can't let you stop what I've worked so hard to build."

Jimmy James needed to buy more time. "You personally extend an invitation to people you know have expensive jewelry collections. Then you must somehow study what they have and make perfect replicas of the pieces."

"Continue." He crossed his arms as if enjoying this.

"You have someone on the crew who switches the pieces out for you, and the guests never know what happened," Jimmy James continued. "That's what those white gloves I found were for. It was to keep fingerprints off the jewelry."

"Those gloves should have never been found. Some people are so sloppy. They should stick with making jewelry." He pressed his lips together and raised his eyebrows in an annoyed expression.

"If people ever do figure out that their jewelry isn't real, enough time will have passed that they won't realize when the jewelry was switched out," Kenzie said. "Am I right?"

Mr. Robertson scowled. "You're a lot smarter than I gave you credit for. And here I thought it was going to be easy to pull the wool over your eyes. I couldn't have been more wrong."

"Is that why you hired me?" An edge of defensiveness rose in Kenzie's voice. "Because you thought I wouldn't catch on?"

He shrugged. "I figured you were new enough that you wouldn't ask questions. Plus, I made sure there was enough drama onboard to keep you distracted—or so I thought. And Jimmy James over there . . . I figured he'd make a great scapegoat."

"And here I thought it was for my good looks and spotless record," Jimmy James muttered.

"You practically stumbled into our whole scheme. When I heard you were a captain, I knew you'd be perfect."

"You know nothing about him!" Kenzie clenched her fists.

Her defense of him touched Jimmy James. But there was no time for that now.

"How did the senator fit in?" Jimmy James asked, buying more time.

"It was all about the jewelry." His eyes narrowed again. "I was afraid it would draw unnecessary attention to the boat. Instead, all the attention went to them. Scandalous politicians have a way of doing that. And when people heard that the senator had chartered *Almost Paradise*, calls began pouring in."

Another realization hit Jimmy James, this one sent burning hot anger through his veins. "You were the one that set Kenzie adrift . . . you probably hired Dagger Agency to do more dirty work for you."

The Dagger Agency was a less than ethical group of security agents who did whatever was necessary for their payday. Jimmy James had experienced one run-in with them already, and he knew with certainty they weren't the kind of people he admired.

"Actually, I hired someone much closer to do that job, but he failed me." Mr. Robertson narrowed his gaze.

"What do you mean?" Jimmy James had suspected that someone on the boat was in on this. Had he been correct?

More footsteps sounded behind them, and he turned.

Eddie and Sunni stood there.

"You two are both in on this?" Jimmy James muttered. "The chief stew and the first mate?"

"Eddie is actually a fine arts major who's been involved in the jewelry business for a long time," Mr. Robertson said. "He's a master at what he does. He's the one who makes the replicas, and Sunni helps switch them out."

"We almost got caught this week when Mrs. Abernathy noticed that her necklace was missing before we could replace it." Sunni shrugged.

"I was in the middle of switching it out when she walked into the salon," Eddie explained. "Sunni had to distract her so I could get out of her room. But I managed to make Mrs. Abernathy look like the crazy one."

"And you had access to the security cameras and erased that footage," Jimmy James filled in.

"Bingo!"

"Where did you keep the replicas until you switched them out?" Jimmy James asked.

"In the owner's closet." He nodded toward the locked closet in the distance.

"But the police searched that place during one of our charters . . ." Kenzie said.

"I have two boxes under the floorboards. They're integrated to ensure no one will find them."

Mr. Robertson certainly had thought everything through.

"Let me guess—Eddie, you were the one someone saw on the boat before we departed? Were you restocking the owner's closet?" Jimmy James asked.

Eddie shrugged. "Maybe."

"You're the one who put me in that boat and sent me out into the ocean, aren't you, Eddie?" Kenzie's jaw jumped as if she could barely withhold her anger.

"Yes, and he's the one that left your cell phone with you." Mr. Robertson scowled at him.

Eddie frowned, sending a fleeting glance to Kenzie—one that almost looked like an apology. "I may be a thief, but I'm not a killer. I couldn't leave you out there with no means to get help."

"If he wasn't so valuable to me, that would have been a grave mistake on his part," Mr. Robertson stated. "He's going to have to work extra hard to make it up to me."

"Do you have my dad?" Kenzie rushed.

Mr. Robertson smirked again. "Let's just say we're keeping an eye on him, just in case we need more leverage."

"You shouldn't have involved him." Kenzie started to lunge forward, but Jimmy James gripped her arm, trying to stop her.

He needed to make sure tempers didn't flare and accelerate anything.

Jimmy James turned back to Mr. Robertson. "What are you going to do with us now? Here we are. We know your secrets. So, what happens next?"

"That's a good question, one I've given a lot of thought to. I actually had two of my security agents come with me so they could help out and make sure no one had a change of heart before the dirty work was done."

Just then two security guards appeared from an adjoining engine room. One held two chains with small anchors on the end. The other displayed his handgun.

As soon as Jimmy James saw the chains, he knew exactly what these guys were planning.

But he couldn't manage to say the words out loud —because the very idea was too horrific.

## CHAPTER FORTY-ONE

AS KENZIE STARED at the weighted chains, cold fear filled her veins. "What are you going to do with those?"

She thought she already knew the answer to that question, but she hoped she was wrong. She *prayed* she was wrong.

"We're going to attach this to your leg." Mr. Robertson nodded to one of the security agents, and the man stepped toward her.

Before the man could reach her, Jimmy James pulled Kenzie behind him. "I don't think so."

"Do you really think you're going to win?" Mr. Robertson stared up at him. "You're outnumbered. And we're the ones with the guns, just in case you need to be reminded."

Jimmy James bristled, all six-plus feet of him rising to full height and his broad chest seeming to stretch even wider. "You're going to have to go through me before you touch her."

"Very well then." Mr. Robertson nodded at his security guards again.

The two men rushed toward Jimmy James. Kenzie stepped back, but one of the engines was behind her and a wall was on the other side. She was trapped.

Jimmy James was the only one who could help her now.

He swung his fist at one of the men, hitting him square in the jaw. The man moaned.

Before Jimmy James could turn, the other guard rammed his fist into Jimmy James' stomach. Jimmy James leaned over, the wind clearly knocked out of him, but quickly righted himself.

Those other two men may be trained in security. But Jimmy James had gone through the school of hard knocks—which might just give him a leg up.

He spread his arms out, and his fists hit both of the men squarely in their jaws.

They quickly recovered and rushed him at the same time, shoving him back toward the wall. Kenzie quickly jumped out of the way.

He hit the wall with an *oof*.

"Jimmy James!" Kenzie started to reach for him.

But he raised his hand, signaling her to stay back.

As Jimmy James rose to full height again, she sensed movement beside her.

She looked over and saw Mr. Robertson dive toward her leg. Before she could move, he snapped the chain around her ankle and locked it in place.

A new sense of dread pooled in her stomach.

This wasn't good. How would she get this thing off?

She knew the truth.

She wouldn't be able to do it . . . not without a key. If she went into the water with this on . . . there was no way she'd survive—not even if Jimmy James jumped in to help her.

---

"KENZIE . . ." Jimmy James saw the chain around her ankle and felt a trace of panic race through him.

That wasn't supposed to happen.

The moment he turned to look, one of the security guards grabbed his arm and rammed his fist into

Jimmy James' stomach again. The air left his lungs. Jimmy James raised his fist to fight back.

Before he could act, the man grabbed the gun from his holster and pointed it at Jimmy James' head. "One more move, and I'll pull the trigger. Understand?"

Jimmy James glanced at Kenzie again, still worried about her.

The situation had certainly just gotten much more dangerous than it was before.

"Let her go," Jimmy James said. "She doesn't have anything to do with this."

Mr. Robertson smirked. "It's too bad she had to get herself involved."

"She didn't get herself involved," Jimmy James said. "She saw something was wrong and looked for answers."

"Exactly. Now she knows too much. Both of you do."

"There has to be another way." As Jimmy James said the words, his mind raced. He had to think of a way out of this.

"Believe me, I've thought all this through. The only way this works for me is if you disappear. I'll tell people the two of you ran off together. Based on your actions over the past few weeks, people will probably believe it. The two of you fell in love and went away to start a new life together. Maybe in the Caribbean."

"No one's going to believe that," Kenzie told him through clenched teeth. "You're going to get caught."

"I have something good going on here. I'm not going to let you ruin it." Mr. Robertson nodded toward the stairs. "Now, get them out there to the deck. We need to get this over with before anyone else returns to the boat."

Jimmy James knew he didn't have much time. He couldn't let Kenzie leave this room or it would all be over.

"You can't kill them—" Eddie stepped forward.

As he said the words, Mr. Robertson backhanded him, and Eddie flew back. Sunni gasped and reached for him.

It was just the distraction Jimmy James needed.

As one of the security guards reached for Jimmy James' ankle, he raised his leg. His knee smashed the man in the face. He then reached forward and knocked the gun away from the other guard.

The security guard's gun fired as it left his hand.

His bullet must have grazed Sunni. She let out a yelp and grasped her shoulder.

"Sunni?" Eddie turned to her.

Jimmy James didn't have time to watch that play out. Instead, he grabbed the gun the man had dropped and turned it on him. As the other security guard pulled his gun, Jimmy James slammed that man's hand into the wall. The weapon teetered to the floor.

"Kenzie, grab it!" he yelled.

With trembling hands, Kenzie reached down. Her fingers gripped the gun and she raised it, a tentative look on her face.

Mr. Robertson's eyes widened as he took a step back. "You're not going to win this."

"I'm not?" Jimmy James asked.

At that moment, police officers flooded down the stairs.

Backup was here.

Thank goodness.

Now Jimmy James just needed to get that anchor off Kenzie's ankle. With their string of bad luck, she might somehow slip and end up in the water anyway.

He couldn't let that happen.

# CHAPTER FORTY-TWO

KENZIE WATCHED as one of the cops used a key they'd taken from Mr. Robertson to get the lock from the chain around her ankle. As soon as the chain released from her leg, a sense of relief filled her.

Maybe in more ways than one.

What kind of weights and burdens had she been carrying around with her for so long? Being released from them felt like she had a chance at a new start.

She had some amends to make, but she didn't regret setting out on her own. She'd done this for her own good.

One of the medics helped her rise to her feet. As she did, she winced. Her ankle still didn't feel great, but at least she didn't have an anchor wrapped around her other leg anymore.

She reached for the wall to steady herself when Jimmy James appeared.

In two steps, he wrapped his arms around her waist. He pulled her to him in a bear hug so tight she could hardly breathe. But she didn't mind.

What really mattered was that she was okay. As was her father.

Cassidy had called a few moments ago and told her that her dad was now at the police station up in the mountains of Virginia. Local police had found Dr. Anderson and brought him in before any of Robertson's men could harm him.

"You're better than any action hero I've ever seen," she murmured in Jimmy James' ear.

"You think? I didn't feel like an action star."

"Believe me when I say you looked like one." She pulled away from him, and they shared a grin. But her arms remained around his neck, and her thumb gently stroked his cheek. "Thank you for what you did. If you hadn't acted . . ."

He pulled her close again. "I thought I was going to lose you. I've thought that more than once over the past week, and I don't like it."

"I don't like it either. Believe me."

They held each other for several minutes, ignoring the police officers milling around.

A few minutes later, Jimmy James pulled back enough to look her in the eye. "Do you remember what we talked about after our last charter? When I told you that I wanted to prove to you how much I cared about you?"

"I do." Kenzie remembered the conversation like it was just yesterday. Jimmy James had taken her to a sandbar in the middle of the water to watch the sunset. The moment was forever etched into her mind.

"I meant those words, Kenzie. I want to do whatever I can to show you how much I care about you."

"I think you've proven that time and time again." Kenzie reached up and planted a long kiss on his lips.

As they pulled away, Jimmy James looked deeply into her eyes, his gaze probing hers. "I do have one question for you."

"What's that?"

"What were you really doing at the pawnshop back in Charleston?"

Her eyelids fluttered a few times as she seemed to process his question. "I wanted to see how much my earrings were worth, just like I told you."

"But those earrings are special to you. Why would you even think about pawning them?"

"I knew your dad needed some cash for his medical bills, and I didn't want you to sacrifice all the money you've been saving for your boat."

His breath caught as realization seemed to fill his gaze. "Kenzie . . . I wouldn't want you to do that for me."

"I know. You didn't ask me to do it. But I wanted to. I'm sorry it didn't work out."

"I have a feeling these guys took your real earrings and switched them out with these fakes. With any luck, you'll be able to get them back."

"I would love to have them back. Don't get me wrong. But the most important things in life aren't things."

"I couldn't agree more." His voice dropped lower. "Thank you for even considering making that sacrifice for me. I can't say that about very many people in my life. It means the world to me to know you'd give up something so valuable to you just so my dreams might come true."

"I guess that's what you do when you're in love with someone . . ."

He raised his eyebrows. "In love?"

She grinned. "I can say without a doubt that I'm definitely falling for you, Jimmy James Gamble."

"Funny you say that . . . because I'm falling for you too."

Their lips met again in another long kiss . . . one Kenzie hoped was one of many more to come.

## EPILOGUE

A WEEK LATER, Kenzie stood on the dock of the Lantern Beach Marina as the sun set in the distance, turning the sky a coral color. She stared at the array of sailboats and fishing boats in front of her. At the very end of the dock, sat a new boat that hadn't been there before.

*Diamond of the Seas.*

The superyacht was going to be her home for the next three months.

Jimmy James stepped behind her. He wrapped his arms around her waist as he nuzzled her neck. "What are you thinking about?"

"I'm thinking about how excited I am to start fresh on *Diamond of the Seas.*"

"I'm pretty excited about that too."

Kenzie turned until they faced each other, Jimmy James' arms still around her waist. "The best part is that I get to be with you, Captain Gamble."

He grinned. "I couldn't agree more."

Mr. Abernathy had decided to buy his own yacht. After he heard what happened on *Almost Paradise*, he'd asked Jimmy James to be the captain and if Kenzie would be chief stew. They'd both said yes.

Even better, Kenzie's dad had come down to Lantern Beach a few days ago and apologized to Jimmy James for making such a harsh judgment call on him. Dr. Anderson had said he could see how much Jimmy James cared about Kenzie and how much Kenzie cared about Jimmy James. He thanked Jimmy James for taking care of Kenzie and gave them his blessing.

When Kenzie's dad had heard about the medical bills Jimmy James' father was facing, Dr. Anderson made a call to an organization he'd worked with before. That organization helped pay off part of those medical bills. Kenzie's father had paid for the remaining bills as his way of saying thank you to Jimmy James for saving his daughter—more than one time.

Meanwhile, Mr. Robertson and his guards were in jail, as were Eddie and Sunni. They had a whole scheme worked out to swindle people of their real jewelry and to leave high-quality replicas behind. Eddie was a very talented jewelry maker, and his work probably wouldn't have been discovered for months. The scheme had been nearly perfect. But Kenzie was grateful they'd discovered what was going on before more jewelry could be stolen.

Jimmy James pushed Kenzie's hair behind her ear as he tenderly gazed at her. "Let's sail away together. You and me."

"I can't think of anything I'd rather do. I'm just praying things will be different on this boat."

"No more trying to solve any crimes?"

She grinned. "Exactly."

"I'm hoping for the same."

Kenzie brushed her hand across Jimmy James' cheek. The affection she felt for this man surpassed anything she ever thought she would experience. Now, she couldn't imagine her future without him.

"I love you, Jimmy James."

A smile spread across his face. "I love you too, Kenzie Anderson."

Their lips met in another kiss.

She couldn't help but think their relationship was a lot like a diamond. She knew it was real because of the imperfections.

It had taken a wakeup call—a mayday of sorts—for her to realize that what she wanted in life was standing right in front of her. Somehow, she knew she and Jimmy James would be a great team when it came to navigating their futures.

---

If you enjoyed this book, please consider leaving a review.

# ALSO BY CHRISTY BARRITT:

OTHER BOOKS IN THE LANTERN
BEACH SERIES:

LANTERN BEACH MYSTERIES

**Hidden Currents**

*You can take the detective out of the investigation, but you can't take the investigator out of the detective.* A notorious gang puts a bounty on Detective Cady Matthews's head after she takes down their leader, leaving her no choice but to hide until she can testify at trial. But her temporary home across the country on a remote North Carolina island isn't as peaceful as she initially thinks. Living under the new identity of Cassidy Livingston, she struggles to keep her investigative skills tucked away, especially after a body washes ashore. When local police bungle the murder investigation, she can't resist stepping in. But

Cassidy is supposed to be keeping a low profile. One wrong move could lead to both her discovery and her demise. Can she bring justice to the island . . . or will the hidden currents surrounding her pull her under for good?

**Flood Watch**

*The tide is high, and so is the danger on Lantern Beach.* Still in hiding after infiltrating a dangerous gang, Cassidy Livingston just has to make it a few more months before she can testify at trial and resume her old life. But trouble keeps finding her, and Cassidy is pulled into a local investigation after a man mysteriously disappears from the island she now calls home. A recurring nightmare from her time undercover only muddies things, as does a visit from the parents of her handsome ex-Navy SEAL neighbor. When a friend's life is threatened, Cassidy must make choices that put her on the verge of blowing her cover. With a flood watch on her emotions and her life in a tangle, will Cassidy find the truth? Or will her past finally drown her?

**Storm Surge**

*A storm is brewing hundreds of miles away, but its effects are devastating even from afar.* Laid-back, loose, and light: that's Cassidy Livingston's new motto. But when a makeshift boat with a bloody cloth inside washes ashore near her oceanfront home, her detective instincts shift into gear . . . again. Seeking clues isn't the only thing on her mind—romance is heating up with next-door neighbor and former Navy SEAL Ty Chambers as well. Her heart wants the love and stability she's longed for her entire life. But her hidden identity only leads to a tidal wave of turbulence. As more answers emerge about the boat, the danger around her rises, creating a treacherous swell that threatens to reveal her past. Can Cassidy mind her own business, or will the storm surge of violence and corruption that has washed ashore on Lantern Beach leave her life in wreckage?

**Dangerous Waters**

*Danger lurks on the horizon, leaving only two choices: find shelter or flee.* Cassidy Livingston's new identity has begun to feel as comfortable as her favorite sweater. She's been tucked away on Lantern Beach for weeks, waiting to testify against a deadly gang, and is settling in to a new life she wants to last forever. When she thinks she spots someone malevolent from her past, panic swells inside her. If an enemy has found her, Cassidy won't be the only one who's a target. Everyone she's come to love will also be at risk. Dangerous waters threaten to pull her into an overpowering chasm she may never escape. Can Cassidy survive what lies ahead? Or has the tide fatally turned against her?

**Perilous Riptide**

Just when the current seems safer, an unseen danger emerges and threatens to destroy everything. When Cassidy Livingston finds a journal hidden deep in the recesses of her ice cream truck, her curiosity kicks into high gear. Islanders suspect that Elsa, the journal's owner, didn't die accidentally. Her final entry indicates their suspicions might be correct and that what Elsa observed on her final night may have led to her demise. Against the advice of Ty Chambers, her former Navy SEAL boyfriend, Cassidy taps into her detective skills and hunts for answers. But her search only leads to a skeletal body and trouble for both of them. As helplessness threatens to drown her, Cassidy is desperate to turn back time. Can Cassidy find what she needs to navigate the perilous situation? Or will the riptide surrounding her threaten everyone and everything Cassidy loves?

**Deadly Undertow**

The current's fatal pull is powerful, but so is one detective's will to live. When someone from Cassidy Livingston's past shows up on Lantern Beach and warns her of impending peril, opposing currents collide, threatening to drag her under. Running would be easy. But leaving would break her heart. Cassidy must decipher between the truth and lies, between reality and deception. Even more importantly, she must decide whom to trust and whom to fear. Her life depends on it. As danger rises and answers surface, everything Cassidy thought she knew is tested. In order to survive, Cassidy must take drastic measures and end the battle against the ruthless gang DH-7 once and for all. But if her final mission fails, the consequences will be as deadly as the raging undertow.

## LANTERN BEACH ROMANTIC SUSPENSE

**Tides of Deception**

Change has come to Lantern Beach: a new police chief, a new season, and . . . a new romance? Austin Brooks has loved Skye Lavinia from the moment they met, but the walls she keeps around her seem impenetrable. Skye knows Austin is the best thing to ever happen to her. Yet she also knows that if he learns the truth about her past, he'd be a fool not to run. A chance encounter brings secrets bubbling to the surface, and danger soon follows. Are the life-threatening events plaguing them really accidents . . . or is someone trying to send a deadly message? With the tides on Lantern Beach come deception and lies. One question remains—who will be swept away as the water shifts? And will it bring the end for Austin and Skye, or merely the beginning?

## Shadow of Intrigue

For her entire life, Lisa Garth has felt like a supporting character in the drama of life. The designation never bothered her—until now. Lantern Beach, where she's settled and runs a popular restaurant, has boarded up for the season. The slower pace leaves her with too much time alone. Braden Dillinger came to Lantern Beach to try to heal. The former Special Forces officer returned from battle with invisible scars and diminished hope. But his recovery is hampered by the fact that an unknown enemy is trying to kill him. From the moment Lisa and Braden meet, danger ignites around them, and both are drawn into a web of intrigue that turns their lives upside down. As shadows creep in, will Lisa and Braden be able to shine a light on the peril around them? Or will the encroaching darkness turn their worst nightmares into reality?

**Storm of Doubt**

A pastor who's lost faith in God. A romance writer who's lost faith in love. A faceless man with a deadly obsession. Nothing has felt right in Pastor Jack Wilson's world since his wife died two years ago. He hoped coming to Lantern Beach might help soothe the ragged edges of his soul. Instead, he feels more alone than ever. Novelist Juliette Grace came to the island to hide away. Though her professional life has never been better, her personal life has imploded. Her husband left her and a stalker's threats have grown more and more dangerous. When Jack saves Juliette from an attack, he sees the terror in her gaze and knows he must protect her. But when danger strikes again, will Jack be able to keep her safe? Or will the approaching storm prove too strong to withstand?

**Winds of Danger**

Wes O'Neill is perfectly content to hang with his friends and enjoy island life on Lantern Beach.

Something begins to change inside him when Paige Henderson sweeps into his life. But the beautiful newcomer is hiding painful secrets beneath her cheerful facade. Police dispatcher Paige Henderson came to Lantern Beach riddled with guilt and uncertainties after the fallout of a bad relationship. When she meets Wes, she begins to open up to the possibility of love again. But there's something Wes isn't telling her—something that could change everything. As the winds shift, doubts seep into Paige's mind. Can Paige and Wes trust each other, even as the currents work against them? Or is trouble from the past too much to overcome?

**Rains of Remorse**

A stranger invades her home, leaving Rebecca Jarvis terrified. Above all, she must protect the baby growing inside her. Since her estranged husband died suspiciously six months earlier, Rebecca has been determined to depend on no one but herself. Her chivalrous new neighbor appears to be an answer to prayer. But who is Levi Stoneman really? Rebecca wants to believe he can help her, but she can't ignore her instincts. As danger closes in, both Rebecca and Levi must figure out whom they can trust. With Rebecca's baby coming soon, there's no time to waste. Can the truth prevail . . . or will remorse overpower the best of intentions?

## Torrents of Fear

The woman lingering in the crowd can't be Allison . . . can she? Because Allison was pronounced dead six years ago. Musician Carter Denver knows only one person who's capable of helping him find answers: Sadie Thompson, his estranged best friend and someone who also knew Allison. He needs to know if he's losing his mind or if Allison could have survived her car accident. Could Allison really be alive? If so, why is she trying to harm Carter and Sadie? As the two try to find answers, can Sadie keep her feelings for Carter hidden? Could he ever care for her, or is the man of her dreams still in love with the woman now causing his nightmares?

## LANTERN BEACH PD

### On the Lookout

When Cassidy Chambers accepted the job as police chief on Lantern Beach, she knew the island had its secrets. But a suspicious death with potentially far-reaching implications will test all her skills

—and threaten to reveal her true identity. Cassidy enlists the help of her husband, former Navy SEAL Ty Chambers. As they dig for answers, both uncover parts of their pasts that are best left buried. Not everything is as it seems, and they must figure out if their John Doe is connected to the secretive group that has moved onto the island. As facts materialize, danger on the island grows. Can Cassidy and Ty discover the truth about the shadowy crimes in their cozy community? Or has darkness permanently invaded their beloved Lantern Beach?

**Attempt to Locate**

A fun girls' night out turns into a nightmare when armed robbers barge into the store where Cassidy and her friends are shopping. As the situation escalates and the men escape, a massive manhunt launches on Lantern Beach to apprehend the dangerous trio. In the midst of the chaos, a potential foe asks for Cassidy's help. He needs to find his sister who fled from the secretive Gilead's Cove community on the island. But the more Cassidy learns about the seemingly untouchable group, the more her unease grows. The pressure to solve both cases continues to mount. But as the gravity of the situation rises, so does the danger. Cassidy is determined to protect the island and break up the cult . . . but doing so might cost her everything.

## First Degree Murder

Police Chief Cassidy Chambers longs for a break from the recent crimes plaguing Lantern Beach. She simply wants to enjoy her friends' upcoming wedding, to prepare for the busy tourist season about to slam the island, and to gather all the dirt she can on the suspicious community that's invaded the town. But trouble explodes on the island, sending residents—including Cassidy—into a squall of uneasiness. Cassidy may have more than one enemy plotting her demise, and the collateral damage seems unthinkable. As the temperature rises, so does the pressure to find answers. Someone is determined that Lantern Beach would be better off without their new police chief. And for Cassidy, one wrong move could mean certain death.

## Dead on Arrival

With a highly charged local election consuming the community, Police Chief Cassidy Chambers braces herself for a challenging day of breaking up petty conflicts and tamping down high emotions. But when widespread food poisoning spreads among potential voters across the island, Cassidy smells something rotten in the air. As Cassidy examines every possibility to uncover what's going on, local enigma Anthony Gilead again comes on her radar. The man is running for mayor and his cult-like following is growing at an alarming rate. Cassidy feels certain he has a spy embedded in her inner circle. The problem is that her pool of suspects gets deeper every day. Can Cassidy get to the bottom of what's eating away at her peaceful island home? Will voters turn out despite the outbreak of illness plaguing their tranquil town? And the even bigger question: Has darkness come to stay on Lantern Beach?

## Plan of Action

*A missing Navy SEAL. Danger at the boiling point. The ultimate showdown.* When Police Chief Cassidy Chambers' husband, Ty, disappears, her world is turned upside down. His truck is discovered with blood inside, crashed in a ditch on Lantern Beach, but he's nowhere to be found. As they launch a manhunt to find him, Cassidy discovers that someone on the island has a deadly obsession with Ty. Meanwhile, Gilead's Cove seems to be imploding. As danger heightens, federal law enforcement officials are called in. The cult's growing threat could lead to the pinnacle standoff of good versus evil. A clear plan of action is needed or the results will be devastating. Will Cassidy find Ty in time, or will she face a gut-wrenching loss? Will Anthony Gilead finally be unmasked for who he really is and be brought to justice? Hundreds of innocent lives are at stake . . . and not everyone will come out alive.

## LANTERN BEACH BLACKOUT

### Dark Water

Colton Locke can't forget the black op that went terribly wrong. Desperate for a new start, he moves to Lantern Beach, North Carolina, and forms Blackout, a private security firm. Despite his hero status, he can't erase the mistakes he's made. For the past year, Elise Oliver hasn't been able to shake the feeling that there's more to her husband's death than she was told. When she finds a hidden box of his personal possessions, more questions—and suspicions—arise. The only person she trusts to help her is her husband's best friend, Colton Locke. Someone wants Elise dead. Is it because she knows too much? Or is it to keep her from finding the truth? The Blackout team must uncover dark secrets hiding beneath seemingly still waters. But those very secrets might just tear the team apart.

## Safe Harbor

Guilt over past mistakes haunts former Navy SEAL Dez Rodriguez. When he's asked to guard a pop star during a music festival on Lantern Beach, he's all set for what he hopes is a breezy assignment. Bree hasn't found fame to be nearly as fulfilling as she dreamed. Instead, she's more like a carefully crafted character living out a pre-scripted story. When a stalker's threats become deadly, her life—and career—are turned upside down. From the start, Bree sees her temporary bodyguard as a player, and Dez sees Bree as a spoiled rich girl. But when they're thrown together in a fight for survival, both must learn to trust. Can Dez protect Bree—and his carefully guarded heart? Or will their safe harbor ultimately become their death trap?

## Ripple Effect

Griff McIntyre never expected his ex-wife and three-year-old daughter to come to Lantern Beach. After an abduction attempt, they're desperate for safety. Now Griff's not letting either of them out of his sight. Bethany knows Griff is the only one who can protect them, despite the fact that he broke her heart. But she'll do anything to keep her daughter safe—even if it means playing nicely with a man she can't stand. As peril ripples through their lives, Griff and Bethany must work together to protect their daughter. But an unseen enemy wants something from them . . . and will stop at nothing to get it. When disaster strikes, can Griff keep his family safe? Or will past mistakes bring the ultimate failure?

**Rising Tide**

Benjamin James knows there's a traitor within his former command. The rest of his team might even think it's him. As danger closes in, he must clear himself and stop a deadly plot by a dangerous terrorist group. All CJ Compton wanted was a new start after her career ended under suspicion. Working as the house manager for private security group Blackout seems perfect. But there's more trouble here than what she left behind. As the tide rushes in, the stakes continue to rise. If the Blackout team fails, it's not just Lantern Beach at stake—it's the whole country. Can Benjamin and CJ overcome their differences and work together to find the truth?

# LANTERN BEACH BLACKOUT: THE NEW RECRUITS

## Rocco

Former Navy SEAL and new Blackout recruit Rocco Foster is on a simple in and out mission. But the operation turns complicated when an unsuspecting woman wanders into the line of fire. Peyton Ellison's life mission is to sprinkle happiness on those around her. When a cupcake delivery turns into a fight for survival, she must trust her rescuer— a handsome stranger—to keep her safe. Rocco is determined to figure out why someone is targeting Peyton. First, he must keep the intriguing woman safe and earn her trust. But threats continue to pummel them as incriminating evidence emerges and pits them against each other. With time running out, the two must set aside both their growing attraction and their doubts about each other in order to work together. But the perilous facts they discover leave them wondering what exactly the truth is . . . and if the truth can be trusted.

## Axel

*Women are missing. Private security firm Blackout must find them before another victim disappears.* Axel

Hendrix likes to live on the edge. That's why being a Navy SEAL suited him so well. But after his last mission, he cut his losses and joined Blackout instead. His team's latest case involves an undercover investigation on Lantern Beach. Olivia Rollins came to the island to escape her problems—and danger. When trouble from her past shows up in town, she impulsively blurts she's engaged to Axel, the womanizing man she's seen while waitressing. Now, she may not be the only one in danger. So could Axel. Axel knows Olivia might be his chance to find answers and that acting like her fiancé is the perfect cover for his latest assignment. But he doesn't like throwing Olivia into the middle of such a dangerous situation. Nor is he comfortable with the feelings she stirs inside him. With Olivia's life—as well as both their hearts—on the line, Axel must uncover the truth and stop an evil plan before more lives are destroyed.

**Beckett**

*When the daughter of a federal judge is abducted, private security firm Blackout must find her.* Psychologist Samantha Reynolds doesn't know why someone is targeting her. Even after a risky mission to save her, danger still lingers. She's determined to use her insights into the human mind to help decode the deadly clues being left in the wake of her rescue. Former Navy SEAL Beckett Jones needs to figure out who's responsible for the crimes hounding Sami. He's not sure why he's so protective of the woman he rescued, but he'll do anything to keep her safe— even if it means risking his heart. As the body count rises, there's no room for error. Beckett and Sami must both tear down the careful walls they've built around themselves in order to survive. If they don't figure out who's responsible, the madman will continue his death spree . . . and one of them might be next.

**Gabe**

When former Navy SEAL and current Blackout operative Gabe Michaels is almost killed in a hit-and-run, the aftermath completely upends his life. He's no longer safe—and he's not the only one. Dr. Autumn Spenser came to Lantern Beach to start fresh. But while treating Gabe after his accident, she senses there's more to what happened to him than meets the eye. When she digs deeper into his past, she never expects to be drawn into a deadly dilemma. Gabe has been infatuated with the pretty doctor since the day they met. Now, can he keep her from harm? Could someone out of his league ever return his feelings or will her past hurts keep them apart? As danger continues to pummel them, Gabe and Autumn are thrown together in a quest to find answers. More important than their growing attraction, they must stay alive long enough to stop the person desperate to destroy them.

# ABOUT THE AUTHOR

*USA Today* has called Christy Barritt's books "scary, funny, passionate, and quirky."

Christy writes both mystery and romantic suspense novels that are clean with underlying messages of faith. Her books have won the Daphne du Maurier Award for Excellence in Suspense and Mystery, have been twice nominated for the Romantic Times Reviewers' Choice Award, and have finaled for both a Carol Award and Foreword Magazine's Book of the Year.

She is married to her Prince Charming, a man who thinks she's hilarious—but only when she's not trying to be. Christy is a self-proclaimed klutz, an avid music lover who's known for spontaneously bursting into song, and a road trip aficionado.

When she's not working or spending time with her family, she enjoys singing, playing the guitar, and exploring small, unsuspecting towns where people have no idea how accident-prone she is.

Find Christy online at:
   www.christybarritt.com
   www.facebook.com/christybarritt
   www.twitter.com/cbarritt

Sign up for Christy's newsletter to get information on all of her latest releases here: **www.christybarritt.com/newsletter-sign-up/**

**If you enjoyed this book, please consider leaving a review.**

Made in the USA
Middletown, DE
19 September 2024

61094343R00198